Assignment Paris

Anne Kimbell

iUniverse, Inc.
New York   Bloomington

Assignment Paris

iUniverse books may be ordered through booksellers or by contacting:

iUniverse
1663 Liberty Drive
Bloomington, IN 47403
www.iuniverse.com
1-800-Authors (1-800-288-4677)

Because of the dynamic nature of the Internet, any Web addresses or links contained in this book may have changed since publication and may no longer be valid. The views expressed in this work are solely those of the author and do not necessarily reflect the views of the publisher, and the publisher hereby disclaims any responsibility for them.

ISBN: 978-1-4502-5888-3 (sc)
ISBN: 978-1-4502-5889-0 (ebk)

Printed in the United States of America

iUniverse rev. date: 10/12/2010

Chapter One

Janine Simms, a tall, silver blond, CIA operative, was pushed abruptly from behind, causing her to stumble on a Paris street, and dive for a basket holding her recently purchased breakfast croissants. At the same time, someone yanked violently at the black leather handbag slung over her shoulder. She turned to face her assailant, ready to kick him where it hurt, and looked down into the faces of two dark skinned teen-age boys. One was holding her purse above his head by its broken strap. The other was hastily picking up the croissants and fruit and stuffing them into his shirt. Janine wasn't sure if she was angrier about her purse or her breakfast. She grabbed the taller boy by the shoulders and plunged her knee into his chest. He yelped in pain but clung determinedly to her purse, shouting a curse at her in Arabic, which Janine understood. "Would you say that to your mother?" she snarled back at him, in perfect colloquial Arabic.

Janine Simms had been strolling down the Rue Belle Chasse in Paris, with a basket of fresh fruit and croissants on her arm. She had smiled at passers by and inhaled the air of the most beautiful city in the world. After assignments in Chad and Tunisia, at last she was home with a chance to use her own apartment in the quiet residential area of Belle Chasse, bought with so much hope years before. The fact that she was the only woman in an all male CIA office no longer concerned her. She had won her spurs with excellent performances in both Chad and Tunisia. Now she was looking forward to some interesting assignments in this lovely city. This sudden attack was a blot on her first perfect morning in her new neighborhood.

The boy understood her Arabic, looked stunned, but held on to her purse as though his life depended on it. As he continued to berate her, she recognized his accent as Algerian. He looked wildly over his shoulder as a gendarme guarding one of the nearby embassies arrived to take charge. Janine was relieved to see the officer, as she had no authority to make arrests in this country, and these boys were clearly on their way to bigger things if not stopped now. The gendarme whistled for support, and the two boys were soon in the custody of policemen who looked as though they had seen this sort of thing before, but not in this upper class neighborhood.

Janine noticed that the younger of the two boys was clutching his shirt, hanging on to the bakery items and fruit that he had stolen. His face was dirty and his clothes ragged. Janine told the policemen that she had never seen either of the boys before.

And she had no idea why they had attacked her. "These Algerian brats are getting braver and braver since al Qaida has begun to operate in their country," the gendarme replied. "They all think that they are future terrorists now. Stealing baguettes is just the first step. The next one will be stealing machine guns." He shook the boy roughly and handed Janine back her purse. "We will take them were they can't cause any more trouble," he said, dragging the boys away toward the local police station.

Janine was shaken. She had reacted instinctively, protecting her belongings. But the fact that the boys were so young and obviously hungry troubled her. She had just been assigned to keep an eye on Algerian settlers in Paris, who might have leanings toward al Qaida. It seemed a daunting task and one that she was not eager to take on. It was another one of the kind of assignments that the 'boys' in the office loved to hand out to her. Topical enough so that it seemed to suit her facility with Arabic and her experience in North Africa, but at the same time fraught with booby traps to her career. She had hoped to spend a few quiet years in her beloved Paris before shipping back to the states for a desk job and eventual retirement. Hopefully, right back here to her cozy apartment on Rue Belle Chasse in Paris.

The thought of the two Algerian teenagers troubled her as she climbed the three flights of stairs to her apartment, which the French called a 'Pied a Terre,' a foothold on the earth, which is exactly how Janine thought about it. During her last assignment in Chad she had thought of it often, and it now contained mementoes of her many assignments. There was even an elephant's foot just inside the door that someone at the American Embassy had given her as a joke just before she left Chad. Even though she abhorred the killing of elephants, she kept it as a sentimental reminder of her time in that desert country.

She stored what was left of her shopping in her tiny fridge. The French certainly didn't believe in mammoth refrigerators with ice machines, and she sometimes regretted not importing one from the states. But as she poured herself a cold drink, she had other things on her mind. How was she going to go about this next assignment? The recent unexplained car bombings in Algiers had suddenly put Algeria on the radar of the US government. It had been a backwater for years. A half tribal place where the residents spent more time attacking one another than anything else. Tribal skirmishes that hadn't bothered her brethren at the CIA much, until now, when they knew that al Qaida was beginning to stake its claim to the country.

The problem was that Paris was full of Algerians. Many of them products of the Algerian war of the 60's that had sent thousands of white French men and women back to Paris to take up lives in what to them was a foreign country. They had been followed over the years by millions of native Algerians, some as guest workers, some as refugees and some as illegal immigrants.

Now there were second and third generations of these French Algerians who had never seen their country of origin, and for whom it had become increasingly romanticized over the years. Al Qaida played on these sympathies among young Algerians, who spent their time hanging around outside cafes and soccer fields with no jobs and little to do but ferment trouble and dream of being taken to Paradise via a car bomb.

But how was she as a tall, blonde woman, and an American, to gain access to these groups and find out what they were planning? Because that was the task that she had just been assigned. She tucked her short, silver blond hair behind her ears and took another sip of her drink, thinking. She knew several Algerian fruit sellers and the owner of a restaurant she sometimes frequented to enjoy authentic "cous cous." They were older men who hardly looked like terrorists. The woman who cleaned her apartment was Algerian, as were many of the other women she saw around Paris doing menial jobs. They were clothed in traditional garb, sweeping, mopping and speaking to each other their sing song dialect as they worked, invisible to the well dressed Parisians who passed them without a glance.

Janine walked to the window and put her glass on the ledge. She had kicked off her shoes as she entered the apartment and she stretched up now onto her toes, looking down the quiet residential street. Perhaps that was the key. These people were largely invisible. Not worthy of a glance because they were the 'other'. They were just a memory of a long and deadly war that most Frenchmen wanted to forget. A recent book by a retired French general, baring his soul about the brutal torture of Algerian enemy combatants, had stung French society to its very core. 'What bad taste he had exhibited to reveal these things now, when those days and that war was best forgotten,' trumpeted the press. But the secret was that it had not been forgotten. Not by the Algerians who had been talking about it over cups of sweet, black tea for three generations. Teenagers, like the ones who had attacked her today, had grown up on these stories. And attacking a tall, well dressed, American woman was just another way to get even. Just as the car bombs in Algiers were, even though it was their own people who bore most of the brunt of the bombs.

Janine noticed two 'gendarmes' walking together down the street, checking addresses. She had given the police hers, but she assumed that the incident was closed. It was just one of a number of attempted muggings that took place routinely in any large city these days. But they stopped in front of the door to her apartment and rang the bell. She buzzed them in and listened as they clumped up the stairs, their boots echoing in the uncarpeted hallway. They were very polite, especially when they had inspected her official US passport. But they looked carefully around the apartment, taking in its ethnic furnishings and memorabilia.

They asked, in careful French, if she had ever seen either of the boys before, and if there was a reason why they might have attacked her? Janine answered in the negative. Wondering why they were making such an issue about a routine and inept attempt at a mugging. They soon explained. One of the boys had been carrying an illegal firearm, and it had been used recently. The victim of that mugging was dead; he had been a noted newspaper correspondent, killed just a few blocks away from her apartment. Such a thing was unheard of in this neighborhood, where there were many well-protected embassies. Janine nodded thoughtfully. This was one of the reasons that she had chosen the neighborhood. That and its nearness to the Seine and the Quay d'Orsay, as well a number of small shops and bistros. It had seemed a delightfully, secure corner of this great city that she planned to finally call home.

But there really wasn't any security anywhere anymore. Her job taught her that. She had dealt most of her career with the underbelly of society and had been the target of attacks before. It was just that this one had been so unexpected, on her own turf, so to speak. She agreed to accompany the police down to the station and identify the boys as the ones who had attacked her. They seemed in a hurry to do this, as though they wanted to get the affair off their docket and move to something more pressing. So Janine agreed to go with them, hoisting her purse over her shoulder and double locking her door behind her. She hadn't expected to have to do that in Paris and in this neighborhood. But caution prevailed.

Chapter Two

The police station was not unlike a million she had seen before in her career. The two young assailants were easily recognizable by their clothes and their attitude, which was unrepentant. The older one glared at the officer, who was attempting to interrogate him. The boy was continuing to deny that the gun was his. He had "found it on the street," he kept repeating in his broken French. 'He hadn't shot anyone; he was just using it to scare the blond woman. He wanted her money that was all.'

Janine understood what he as saying better than the police sergeant seemed to. The boy spoke in a kind of fractured French mingled with his own Algerian dialect. He insisted that he hadn't done anything with the gun. He and his brother were hungry and just wanted money for food. The younger boy hung his head and looked hopelessly at the floor, one hand clutching his torn shirt, where the croissants were still hidden. Janine identified the boys and then was escorted out of the two-way mirrored room. The boys were to be remanded to the juvenile authorities and a search for the parents or someone responsible for them was underway. Janine's help was no longer needed. The gun complicated matters. Janine would be called if she could offer any further help, the gendarme in charge informed her briskly.

Janine walked onto the Boulevard San Germain, around the corner from the police station. She was troubled. Something about the boy's attitude bothered her, and since he was Algerian that made him and his brother a tiny piece of the puzzle that she was trying to piece together. She ordered an espresso and called her friend Sam, a retired American army colonel from the intelligence service, on her cell phone. He had always been a source of helpful information. He had lived in Paris for years, both in the army and now as a civilian consultant. But he always seemed to stay on top of whatever was happening in the intelligence community.

He said on the phone that he wasn't far away and would join her for coffee in a few minutes. While she waited for him, Janine drank her bitter espresso and thought about the hand that had just been dealt her. It was unusual for her not to know how to begin. The threat of al

Qaida in France was a very new one. But of the five men arrested last week, in an attack on UN Headquarters in Algiers, two were French citizens. That brought the threat very close to home. She perused a newspaper while she waited and noted idly that a jet setting Saudi princess was reported missing, as well as her jewels, from a famous Paris hotel. Janine shook her head in disbelief at the reported value of the jewels. How could any one person own or even wear all of that stuff?

When Sam appeared, seemingly out of nowhere, his rumpled appearance was comforting. He had been in the military so long that he still carried himself like an officer, despite his girth. His wrinkled shirt and jacket patched at the elbows, was a good cover for a retired intelligence officer. He ordered a Merlot and smiled at the waiter, who brought it to his table.

"Too early for whiskey," he said, grinning at Janine. " Even if that's what I really want. Now what can an old retired spy do for you, lovely lady?"

Janine smiled at his approach. They had known each other for years, but Sam just couldn't help flirting with every woman he met, even old friends. It was part of his charm and he used it to the fullest.

"I've been saddled with another tricky assignment," she admitted, finishing the last of her bitter coffee. I was hoping that you might give me some idea as to where to start." She told him that she had been assigned to flush out possible al Qaida leaders in Paris and its environs. Perhaps even in Rouen where the UN bombers were known to have recent contacts. "This is not something that a woman can do too easily and perhaps that's why the 'boys' in the office assigned me to it. They hope that I will give up, retire early and go home to mother."

"Then they don't know you very well," Sam grinned. " I've never known you to give up on an assignment. But this is a tricky one for a beautiful, blonde female. Even if you are fluent in Arabic, and have knocked over more than a few bad guys in your time." He paused and lit an evil smelling pipe, looked around for their waiter, and ordered another glass of wine. "The trouble here is that it could be just about anyone. A quarter of the population of Paris has roots in Algeria, and most of them are still talking about what the French did to them in the Algerian war."

He pulled solemnly on his pipe. "Al Qaida in North Africa is just the latest reincarnation of the Slafist Group for Call and Combat or the GSPC as the French call them. They've been hanging around nursing their collective wounds for years, and the chance to link up with an organized terrorist group is like a shot in the arm to them. But how can you smoke them out in Paris? I haven't a clue. But I may know someone who does. Though he is reluctant at the moment to take on this kind of work". He grinned at Janine impishly, as he finished his 'petit rouge.' "I'll have him get in touch, if he is interested," he said, kissing her breezily on both cheeks in farewell.

Janine lingered over the dregs of her coffee for a few more minutes. She wondered who Sam had in mind. She knew that he had contacts all over Paris and North Africa, because he had been in the business for so long. At this moment, she would take any help that she could get from the rumpled little man or anyone else. She had a feeling that as usual the 'boys' had set her up to fail. The fact that she had gotten a commendation for her last assignment in Chad must really stick in their collective craws.

A dark eyed young woman wearing a head scarf and holding a young boy by the hand sat down despondently near Janine. She was obviously distraught. She ordered a coffee in halting French and an orange soda for the little boy. When the refreshments came she hardly touched her cup while the boy slurped away at his soda, eying Janine curiously. The woman told him in Arabic, not to be rude. Janine smiled and answered. "*malish*, it doesn't matter."

The woman looked startled, hearing Janine speak her language, and then she smiled shyly and hugged the boy closer to her. "We have not been here long. He doesn't know that it is rude here to stare," she said in halting French. Then she smiled shyly, "You are very kind," she said, wiping her eyes with the corner of her scarf, and trying not to embarrass herself further by crying. Then she asked in a soft voice. "Do you know where the police station is?"

Against all of her better instincts, Janine moved closer to the woman and little boy. "Yes, I do. I was just there; it is around the corner from here."

The woman looked stricken. "I have come to get my brother who is in trouble with the police. It seems that he attacked a woman in this neighborhood and tried to rob her. That is not like Salim, he is a good boy, not even thirteen. He tries to be a man by stealing and listening to the words of the dissidents who say that we must rise up and attack the French." She looked closely at Janine. "Do you have children? What would you do with a boy like this? I have a feeling that this is just the beginning of his trouble."

Janine agreed. But she didn't want to worry the woman with her opinion. She asked what neighborhood the woman lived in, and where the boy got his radical instruction. The woman looked furtive. But then she shook her head, sighed and mentioned the name of a well-known mosque on the outskirts of Paris near the '*periferique*,' the ring road that circled the city. "He is supposed to go there to learn the Koran. But I think that he learns many more things. But as a woman, I am unable to stop him." She wiped her eyes again with the end of her scarf and then, with the little boy firmly in tow, moved off toward the police station.

Janine sat silently for a few minutes. The information was valuable and made the mugging almost worth it. Now she had to figure out how to pursue it quietly and on her own.

Chapter Three

The phone rang insistently in Rick Harrison's office. It was his private line and it was Saturday. Thinking that it might be someone from the States inquiring about the company's new Algerian project, he finally picked it up and answered abruptly, "Harrison here."

"Sheppard here" was the military sounding response, and then a voice that he had tried to forget, was inviting him to have 'a late afternoon drink on the rue de la Verite.'

That was how he found himself later face to face with the rumpled DOD officer in an out of the way Paris café, just as the late November sun was setting, talking about Janine.

Sam grinned knowingly. "She got under your skin I see. She has a habit of doing that to men. It must be her 'take no prisoners' attitude and the fact that she is a damn good operative."

"Yeah," Rick answered, taking up his drink, and smiling wryly, "all that and a bit more.
"But what's she up to now?"

"She's being launched into a problem relating to Algeria, and I think that she may be out of her league on this one."

When Rick heard the word 'launch' and 'Algeria" used in the same sentence, he picked up his ears. "We are in the middle of big clean up and development project in Algiers. I don't want the crazy lady anywhere near my project."

"Why don't you tell me about it?" Sam asked lighting one of his evil smelling, black cigarettes.

Rick narrowed his eyes. "The Algerians are set to build a multi-million dollar shopping mall, a huge mosque and apartments along the Bay of Algiers, using their freely flowing petro dollars. One of the major hang-ups is the pollution in Oued El Harrach, a highly toxic river that flows directly into the Bay of Algiers. The pollutants are mostly chemicals that our company, among others, sells to the industries along its banks. We are about to sign a large contract to be the major player in cleaning it up before construction begins."

" What about the recent al Qaida-linked car bombings in Algiers?" Sam asked thoughtfully, nudging the conversation along. "Naturally that has some of the money boys scared. But most of the development dollars are Arab. Our clean-up project is just a small part of the deal." Rick narrowed his eyes through Sam's acrid smoke. "What has this got to do with our friend Janine?" Sam smiled; they had finally gotten to the point that he wanted to explore. "Her bosses in the department have sicked her onto identifying the leadership of Algerian dissidents here in France. It's a strange assignment for a good looking, blond, female agent, wouldn't you agree?"

" So as usual, they have set her up to fail?"

"As usual."

"And what is this supposed to mean to me?"

"Thought you might want to give her a call for old time's sake and fill her in on what you know about the situation. You two might be of help to each other. "Just a thought," Sam said, stubbing out his cigarette, and motioning for '*l 'addition.'*

Rick grinned wryly. The old guy was good. He was a champion manipulator, but seeing Janine again was bait he didn't need. On the other hand, Janine might just be in a position to make his job in Algiers simpler. Or at least what she knew might help his company avoid some pitfalls. It might be worth a phone call. But that was all. No involvement, no sir, not ever again.

****

Sunday morning, after shaving and reading the paper, Rick picked up the phone to call the number Sam had given him for Janine's apartment. Her voice on the answering machine sent a tremor down his spine. He wasn't sure if it was lust or just pure anger. She had dropped him like a hot rock after her assignment in Tunisia was over. But she knew as much as anyone about what was going on in the Magreb, for that reason alone she might be useful to him. But no further involvement. His ex-wife, Melanie, was still bugging him from time to time when she was between husbands or lovers. One crazy lady was all he needed in his life.

But Janine wasn't crazy, he reminded himself. Just the opposite. He left his cell phone number on her recorder, and dressed in sweats for his run along the lower banks of the Seine. This was when he liked Paris the best. Early Sunday morning with the trees still holding on to a few leaves, and the barges along the Seine kicking up brown foam as they sped along to their early morning tourist trap locations. Rick waved to a captain he knew. He has been doing this run every morning for five years and by now most of the boats and their crews were familiar to him. The air was cold and it felt good to have his muscles warming up as he ran. He passed several bums wrapped in blankets and smelling of alcohol and urine, asleep in the sun.

'There but for the grace of God go I,' he thought. His job with the chemical company and his love of Paris were about all that held him together. Since his divorce and his unfortunate run in with Janine five years ago, he had stayed on the straight and narrow, drinking a glass of wine now and then, but that was all. He kept his appetite for the stronger stuff intact, like a hidden virus in his belly. His cell phone vibrated. He ignored it. The run and the freedom of the morning felt too good to interrupt with problems. Let whomever it was leave a message. He would pick it up after his run. He passed the Musee d'Orsay on his left as he ran. Its art deco walls reminding all Paris of a more opulent time. A catch in his side made him stop and touch his toes. The cell phone vibrated again against his hip. He caught it as it almost slid out of his pocket. Before he could think, he was talking to his nemesis, Janine Simms.

Her voice was guarded, but she still sounded as though she had just gotten out of someone's bed. It was a quality of tone that made a man curious about who the other fellow was and where she was sleeping. She cleared that up fast. "Sam said that you wanted to talk to me. Where are you? Do you want to meet?"

Rick grimaced. Typical Sam. He had set things in motion and now he was going to step back and watch the fun. Rick winced at the catch in his side. He was getting too old for this sort of thing. Why didn't he just give up and let middle age catch up with him? But his tone was clipped and business like as he responded. "Sam thought that we might be able to help each other," he said acerbically. "Would you care to meet?"

"Well, it's Sunday," she said softly. "Don't you have plans?"

"Sure, meet me on the Bateau Mouche at dock number ten at noon. We can talk while we look at Paris like tourists. I know the captain, so I can get us a table."

"*D'accord*, ok," Janine said, surprised. She didn't know what she had expected from Rick after five years of not hearing from him. But it certainly wasn't a boat ride on the Seine. However, as security went, it was probably as good a place as any. Arab terrorists probably wouldn't be hanging out or signing up for Sunday brunch on the river, featuring a close up of Isle de la Cite'.

Back in his apartment, Rick showered, shaved, checked his faxes from the states and thought about all the reasons he was crazy to think about hooking up with Janine again. She was smart, sexy, fearless and a lot of trouble to any man she linked up with even for a short time. But this was business. His company was risking a huge amount of credibility bidding on the clean up project in Algiers. If the CIA, through Janine, had any information that would make the job less doomed for failure, which Rick felt in his gut it was, the information was worth exploring.

That is why he showed up early at dock number ten to make sure that he and Janine got a reserved and very quiet table for lunch. Whatever she knew or didn't know at this point he wanted to make sure that their conversation wasn't overheard. The captain gave him a knowing look. "Oh '*les amants*', the lovers," he murmured to Rick, leading him to a very secluded table in the bow of the boat. Rick admired the sun glinting off the bell towers of Notre Dame while he waited for Janine and mentally cursed himself for even thinking about getting involved with her again. But this time it was business and business only. Yeah, right. She had gotten under his skin in a way that no woman had for a long time, and the way she had brushed him off after her assignment in Tunisia was finished still rankled.

He caught her scent before he saw her, a waft of faint jasmine perfume that tinted the air around her. She was dressed in jeans and a red, turtle neck, sweater that set off her silver blonde hair and amber eyes. She smiled brightly and stuck out her hand, as though she was greeting an old friend that she hadn't seen in a long time. Rick ignored the hand and motioned abruptly to the seat opposite him at the table. Janine shrugged and reached for the glass of wine that was waiting at her place. "Thanks for remembering that I like gewertz," she said, sipping her drink, and eyeing him directly over the top of her glass. "It's been a long time."

"I guess that I should say 'too long,' but I really don't feel that way."

" Our old friend Sam working his 'magic' again," she replied, tucking a lock of silver blonde hair behind her ear, adorned with tiny gold hoops that sparkled in the sunlight.

"He thinks that we can help each other."

"And can we?"

"Depends," Rick said squinting against the afternoon sun and taking a slow sip of his wine.

Janine noticed that his face looked even leaner that usual. He had the faint shadow of a beard, as though he had shaved very early or not at all. His gray eyes looked right through her. 'Don't bullshit me,' they seemed to say. 'I've been there before.'

"Well, can we?" Janine repeated, tasting her wine.

When he didn't answer, she continued, "I guess it's a case of you show me yours and I'll show you mine. But at the moment I don't have much to show. Just a bunch of suspicions and the curious disappearance of a Saudi Princess, which may or may not have anything to do with what I'm charged with looking into."

"And what would that be?"

Janine looked out over the water, and spoke softly as a speedboat crashed by, muffling her voice. "Locating Algerian al Qaida operatives in Paris. Smoking out the big boys, so someone can take them out quietly."

Rick grimaced, "Doesn't sound like your kind of job. Why are they sending a woman to do a man's work?"

Janine shrugged. She was still amazingly attractive, though thinner than when he had last seen her. " Some of their contacts may be women. Recently some of the suicide bombers have been. The Saudi women are here in force, shopping up a storm for Paris gowns to wear under their burquas. They are easy enough to contact."

"But for the rest of it, you may need a man."

"Something like that," she nodded. "But what's in it for you?"

Rick decided to level with her. "My company is playing for a very large stake in Algiers, funded by a multi-national company and Saudi and Algerian oil dollars. A continuing replay of the recent bombings, or even worse, could slow the money down or cut it off completely. I need to know whatever you learn."

"And what do I get out of it?"

"As you so aptly put it. 'You show me yours and I'll show you mine' nothing personal,"

He added grimly, signaling the waiter to bring them their first course as the boat slowly pulled away from the dock.

"Sounds like it might turn out to be fun," Janine said, grinning at him over her *sole meuniere.*

Chapter Four

It was dark on the Rue Belle Chasse. Most of the embassies had closed for the night and the only traffic was for the few exclusive small hotels that were nestled back from the street, catering to a very privileged clientele. A man wearing a black jogging suit with the hood pulled up, stood in the shadows across the street, looking up at the dimly lit windows of Janine's apartment. He leaned against the corner of the building, smoking a cigarette, looking as though he were waiting for some one to join him at one of the small restaurants scattered up and down the block. He watched Janine's windows carefully. Occasionally he could see a shadow walking in front of the light. He crossed the street silently and rang her doorbell several times. At first there was no answer. Then her amplified voice came over the intercom asking who was there. He didn't answer, just rang the bell again violently. She responded again, in a more guarded voice this time. He muttered a violent threat in Arabic, hung up, and then walked rapidly across the road, and silently down the street. The first part of his mission accomplished.

Janine finished dressing, but her hands were icy cold. She had heard that accent before, if not the voice itself. She hadn't even begun this mission and already there were threats. How had they found out where she lived? As far as she knew the information was classified. But with the Internet it was almost impossible for anyone to hide anymore. She thought about aborting her plans to attend a public service at the Grand Mosque this evening. It was in the same *arrondissement* where she lived, and a major tourist attraction. If she dressed conservatively and wore a headscarf, she could be taken for a tourist, out for a stroll, not a CIA operative in search of information.

This was just a fishing expedition, and she knew it. But the young Algerian boys who had attacked her, were taking jihad and terrorist instructions somewhere in a mosque. They were clearly learning more than the Quran. She had to start somewhere and the local mosque seemed as good a place as any to begin her search.

As she strolled down the darkening street, she kept her eyes and her head down, like a good Arab woman. But it was difficult to contain her athletic stride. She was alert to listen for anyone following her. She stopped several times to gaze into lighted windows of local bistros crammed with their after work customers. She saw her own image reflected in the lighted windows, but no one else that she could identify. The streets were still lively with shoppers and people returning late from work.

Perhaps whoever rang her bell was looking for someone else. There were a number of apartments occupied by high-class call girls who prided themselves in only servicing diplomats and members of the government, Janine smiled. She hadn't known that when she purchased her *'pied a terre.'* Perhaps that was why the agent who sold it to her had negotiated so hard on the price. He must have thought that she had a 'protector' who was paying the bills.

'No chance of that' Janine thought, tugging her long black coat more securely around her slender frame. The evening was cold, and for the moment she was even glad of the headscarf. It was keeping her ears warm while doing a bit to hide her identity. She knew that this was just a random fishing expedition. But it was hard not to take advantage of the fact that one of the largest mosques in Paris, founded by an Algerian, was in her immediate neighborhood. It was too good an opportunity to miss. Besides she liked to walk in the evening, and this was as good a chance as any to collect her thoughts and plan how she was going to approach this job.

Her stride got shorter as she approached the mosque. Evening prayers were over, but it was still brightly lit. A bulletin board just inside the gate listed classes and other youth activities. She saw that there were a number of study sessions for the Quran, with men's and women's classes indicated at separate times.

'No chance of meeting anyone that way,' she thought. 'So much for adult education.'

A neatly dressed young man approached her slowly. He kept his distance and avoided looking into her eyes. So they both wound up talking to each other's feet. He offered to help her with finding a class if that was what she was interested in. Janine found herself asking about the women's classes, getting times and information about how and when to sign up.

" We are starting another series for women next week. You are fortunate," the young man said solemnly, "but you are not Arab, where does your interest come from?"

" I am a student of all religions," Janine said to him softly in Arabic, keeping her head averted modestly. "It is time that I learned something of the holy Quran."

The young man nodded, seeming to agree with her. But he continued to watch her suspiciously. It was his job to protect this holy place from infidels.

Janine certainly felt like one. She was here under false pretenses and the longer she hesitated the more out of place she felt. The young man's demeanor, though polite, was becoming somewhat hostile.

" I will return at a more appropriate time," Janine said softly. "Thank you for your offer to help me with choosing a class. May I ask your name?"

"Brahim," he said quietly, taking a step toward her.

Janine backed away, feeling foolish. But this was his territory, she had knowingly invaded it, and it was rapidly getting darker. She could hear the voices of other men entering through the ornate gate behind her. She heard the word 'meeting' in Arabic and then an angry voice asking why Brahim was entertaining a woman in this sacred place.

As the young man turned to try to explain her presence as a prospective scholar and possible recruit to Islam, Janine turned, and murmuring an excuse in French, began to inch toward the gate, keeping her head down modestly. Brahim watched her walk away, his eyes full of suspicion.

The men avoided her as though she were a leper come to take refuge in the mosque. They continued their hushed conversations in Arabic, ignoring her presence as she hurried past them into the dark street. She had learned a very important lesson. As a woman she was so unimportant that they didn't even bother to whisper in her presence. So in a sense this was a victory, and a small step in the direction of her investigation. They would never suspect that she was spying on them. And she was sure that this mosque was one of the ones that she was looking for. These men had not come for prayers. They were planning something. The question was how was she going to find out what it was and who was in charge?

****

Rick cursed himself as he finished dressing for his evening meeting with his company managers. How had he let himself get involved with this woman again? She was nothing but trouble, always had been and always would be. Since their affair in Tunisia five years ago, he had studiously managed not to have any more contact with her. He knew how important her career was to her, and to what lengths she would go to have a success in anything she started. The men in her agency knew it too, and that was probably why they continually saddled her with difficult and dangerous assignments.

But this one was a dead end for a woman, even a woman as bright and determined as Janine. The question was, how much did he really want to get involved with her again even to help complete this very important Algerian deal?

He had an urge to call her. Then quickly squashed it. The situation in Algiers was heating up. With a relatively stable government and gushing oil reserves, the country was on the brink of a real economic take off, if they could keep the terrorists at bay. Al Qaida would like nothing better than to drag the country back into the dark ages. Already some of the top brass in his company were getting nervous. Hence tonight's hastily called meeting. It required a very large investment of men and material to get the clean up job done. And there wasn't a great deal of time. If he could pull this one off, it could cement his career and his retirement. Particularly, since his son Robbie seemed set on going to graduate school at Harvard to major in philosophy. Paying for what Rick privately thought of as Robbie's extended childhood, was going to cost money. Money that he didn't have at the moment.

But he couldn't put Janine completely out of his thoughts as he finished dressing. He just kept the more lascivious ones at bay, while he tried to figure out how they were going to work together again without ending up in bed. The prone position was not the best one for cold-blooded calculation of how they, single-handed, were going to outwit al Qaida in Algiers.

Chapter Five

Janine walked slowly back toward her apartment, still lost in thought. She had almost too easily found a clue this evening at the Grand Mosque. But it was one that she wasn't quite sure how to follow up. She could certainly enroll in a class. Her Arabic was more than sufficient, and if they were really looking to enlarge the numbers of believers, the classes might even be taught in French. Brahim hadn't seemed too surprised at her interest and might have continued to encourage her, if his male friends hadn't shown up.

She removed the headscarf and shook out her short silver-blonde hair. She was hungry and, as usual, there was little to eat in her tiny refrigerator. She had thought when she bought the *pied a terre* that she would replace the 'fridge' and stock it for all emergencies. But she had traveled so much since returning to Paris that the time or opportunity hadn't come up. So it was either eat really old cheese and some stale crackers, or stop in one of the local bistros for what passed for bar food in Paris.

El Cid, the romantically named sandwich and coffee shop on the corner of her street was just about to close its doors. But the owner recognized her and, giving a resigned shrug, let her in and ushered her to the corner seat she often chose. It featured mirrors on both sides of the table that allowed her to see down the street in both directions. It was her long-standing habit to watch her back, even in her own neighborhood in Paris. She quickly ordered a *'Croque Monsieur'*, a fancy name for what was essentially a grilled cheese sandwich, and a glass of the house white wine. Nodding approvingly, the owner brought it to her in record time.

She was alone in the café except for an elderly couple finishing their simple supper. The owner, a robust man in his fifties with a guttural French accent, was busy behind the bar polishing glasses, while berating the one waitress for being late that evening. Janine smiled, some things never changed. She could remember similar conversations from her college days as wait staff in the student union. As she bit into her *'Croque Monsieur'*, she caught movement out of the corner of her eye. A man was standing outside the window staring in at her. Because of the reflection of the outside lights, she couldn't see his face, but the light reflected off his silver belt buckle and his white running shoes. As she glanced at him, he moved back out of her line of sight. But she was sure that he was still there, watching her as she finished her sandwich and slowly sipped her wine.

Now she was the last customer in the café. The elderly couple had departed with much hustling on of coats and many thanks to the café owner. He responded graciously, but kept his eyes on Janine's table. He was obviously anxious for her to leave so that he could close for the night. Janine was in total sympathy, but she wanted to keep an eye on the man outside the window. So she sipped her wine slowly and ignored *l'addition* for a few minutes when it came. She wasn't armed. The French police frowned on civilians carrying weapons, except in extraordinary cases. She wasn't in a hurry to find out why this man was watching her. She finished her wine and stood up, walking slowly to the bar to pay her bill. Then she sauntered back to her table, ostensibly to leave a tip. When she glanced through the window, a crowd of students was coming down the street, singing and cheering loudly for their rugby team. Her observer was not in sight.

Janine took advantage of the students to slip out of the café and mingle with them till they got to the front door of her apartment building. She gave a silent cheer for their team as she opened the door rapidly and slipped inside. Glancing back over her shoulder, she saw the street lamp illumine a man dressed in a leather jacket and white athletic shoes. He was staring at her from the other side of the street. And it was clear that he wanted her to see him and to know that she was being watched.

Janine hurried up the stairs to her apartment and closed and locked the door. She had always felt safe in this neighborhood. But something unusual was going on. Someone wanted her to know that she was being observed. The man was making no effort to hide himself. In fact, he wanted her to be aware of him. She thought of the mysterious ringing of her doorbell earlier. Someone wanted to make her feel threatened here on her own turf in Paris. But who was it and for what reason?

She turned on her small television. French elections were in progress. One of the candidates was revisiting the Algerian war and warning of the possibility of Algerian terrorists in France. The other, a young Moslem woman, was defending the millions of peace loving Algerians, who now made their homes in France and were French citizens. She claimed that they were being unjustly persecuted because of their militant Moslem brothers. Her argument didn't get much applause, but she stuck to her guns. Janine decided that she might be a good person to get to know if the opportunity arose.

Surprising enough the opportunity arose the next morning.

Chapter Six

Two very different women shared the headlines the following morning. Jalila Haddad, the young French Algerian woman from a working class family who had just won an overwhelming vote of confidence to become the government representative for Housing and Welfare. The second, was a follow up piece about the still missing Saudi Princess and her jewelry.

In photographs the two women resembled one another slightly. Both with heart shaped faces and dark hair and eyes. But there the resemblance ended. Jalila had fought her way through the French educational system to graduate with a doctorate in economics. The Saudi Princess was only slightly educated and had spent most of her time in Paris, shopping and attending parties. Her brother, the prince, one of over two hundred and fifty Saudi princes, was worried that she might have been abducted as a threat to the royal family, who were conservative Wahabi Moslems. He was offering a huge reward for any information as to her whereabouts.

Janine sipped her coffee and thought about the difference in the two women. Jalila had struggled up out of the slums of Paris to become a government minister. The Saudi Princess had been surrounded by luxury and seemingly had only used it for her own amusement. But the kidnapping, if that was what it was, was sending a message to someone. Janine wondered who the recipient was meant to be.

Following a hunch, she decided to attend a rally in the 16th *arrondissement*, where Haddad was scheduled to attend a victory celebration in her old neighborhood. It would be a chance to get a look at this extraordinary young woman, and also check out one of the poorer immigrant neighborhoods where young dissidents were recruited. Janine knew that what she was doing was just a fishing expedition. But her instinct told her that something just might turn up to point her in the right direction.

Just then her cell phone rang insistently. Checking the number, she could see that it was the office calling. Since it was Saturday she thought about ignoring it, but her less than privileged status in the office, urged her to answer it. Her boss was on the other line. He was terse as usual.

"What have you got going today?" he said in a voice that passed for casual, but wasn't.

"Following up on something." Janine replied, deliberately evasive.

" Well, the Saudi's have asked for our help in locating her Royal Highness. She was last seen shopping at the Gallerie Lafayette, Boulevard Haussmann near the Opera. Why don't you check it out, and see what you can find."

"Not exactly world class shopping for a princess."

"What can I tell you? Seems like all you women, she likes bargains."

Janine decided not to react to his dismissive tone. Finding out what section of the store the princess had been seen shopping in was her next question, "Then, I'll check it out," she said abruptly and hung up, before she was given any more instructions about how to do her job.

The department store opened at ten. She could get over there and check out the shoe department and still have time to make the rally this afternoon. For some reason, she really wanted to get a look at Haddad and especially the neighborhood that had spawned her. Many of the Algerian immigrants in Paris lived in near poverty and had for three generations. The fact that a woman had arisen from that milieu to become a member of the government was a sort of miracle. Janine liked winners. It would give her a lift just to meet this lady. After she had checked out what the princess had been shopping for at Gallerie Lafayette.

She caught a bus two blocks from her apartment. This time on a Saturday it was a scenic way to get to Place de l'Opera and she had half an hour to kill before the store opened. She loved this time of the morning in Paris. Shoppers were out and the traffic was already snarled as only the French can snarl it. The sidewalk along Boulevard San Germain was already parked solid with small cars vying for position half on and half off the sidewalk. The heady smell of fresh bread drifted out of the neighborhood bakery. Janine bought a buttery croissant and munched on it on her way to the bus stop.

She felt almost carefree, as she had here in her student days. The child of a German mother and an American military father, she had landed at the Sorbonne as an awkward teenager. But she had inhaled the language and the culture, and everything that she had learned in this beautiful city had stood her in good stead in her career in government. Fluent in French and German and her recently honed Arabic, she felt like a citizen of the world. Her desire to join the Central Intelligence Agency had come from an idealistic desire to serve her country and help to preserve some sanity in the world. At the moment, the world seemed to be winning.

She hopped off the bus just in front of the Opera building and took a second to look up at its grand façade. Created by Charles Garnier in 1862, and sometimes compared by the irreverent to a giant wedding cake, it was still one of grand sights of Paris, which did not lack for grand sights. Looking at the posters outside, she decided to indulge herself in a pair of tickets for *La Boheme*. Perhaps she would stun Rick and invite him to go with her one evening. She had treated him pretty badly after Tunisia. Maybe it was time to make amends.

The department store was crowded even at this relatively early hour of the morning. The sidewalk outside was lined with carts advertising specials: miracle silver cleaner, steak knives, and authentic Persian scarves from China. Everything a shopper needed to while away the morning and feel justified at the bargains she'd acquired.

But Janine was not a shopper, and she had urgent business on her mind. She took the elevator up to the shoe department where her boss had informed her that the Princess had last been seen. Had she been abducted from here? No one seemed quite sure. She spied a portly man, in a too tight black suit, in the boot section. Following a hunch, she wandered in his direction, picking up an expensive pair of kid leather boots to admire. The salesman suddenly came to life before her eyes and began to exude an unctuous charm. "Does Madame enjoy the finest leather? Notice how supple it is, how soft to the touch," he burbled in his Marseilles accented French.

Janine murmured something approving, not asking the price. Which the salesman took immediate notice of and appreciated. She asked to see them in her size and in several colors. When he came trotting back laden with boxes, she began to try the boots on slowly, one pair at a time. The she stood up to admire herself in the mirror, nodding approvingly. By now the salesman was practically salivating. "Are these the ones that Princess Saroya purchased?" Janine asked, turning from side to side to admire her profile.

The man looked taken aback. Janine could see that he was hesitating between his pride at having served the Princess and the 'no comment about celebrity customer's policy' that the store management had drummed into his soul. As he hesitated, Janine shook her head and began to remove the boot. "I want the ones that the Princess was interested in," she said in what, for her, passed for a petulant voice. "Those are the only ones that interest me."

The salesman hesitated, torn between duty and making a sale. His greed did him in. Before he could stop himself, he was relating how he had served the princess only yesterday, and how she had almost purchased those very boots, until two men arrived with an urgent message from her brother. Unfortunately she had had to leave without purchasing anything. But he alone had had the honor of serving her, he related smugly.

"Did she go with the men willingly?" Janine asked casually, now pulling on a third pair of boots in a vibrant lipstick red.

The salesman nodded approvingly at her choice, then shook his head sadly. "The Princess did not want to leave before finishing her shopping. But the men insisted rather strongly that she and her lady companion accompany them to their car immediately. Janine could see the scene in her mind's eye. Whoever had come to get Saroya must have been someone that she knew. Otherwise she would not have left with them without a struggle. But that didn't mean that they might have had other things in mind than giving her a message from her brother, who was a well-known Saudi playboy, with lots of international connections in the darker side of business.

At any rate, this was the last place that she had been seen. Her clothes and jewelry had been removed from her hotel room. But her boss had told Janine that no one had seen her return to pack. Janine planned to check out the Ritz hotel later in the day and find out what she could learn from the hotel staff. But in the meantime, she had to avoid purchasing a pair of seven hundred dollar boots, which she knew, regretfully, that the office wouldn't pay for. She smiled at the salesman, trying to let him down gently. "Put these aside for me," she said languidly. " I will come back for them when I've finished the rest of my shopping."

But the salesman had heard that line before. He assured her that the boots looked elegant on her. They made her look just like a princess, but an American one, he said almost stuttering in his anxiety to please his customer. Janine extricated herself as swiftly as she could, jamming on her low-heeled pumps and striding rapidly down an aisle on her way to the elevator. The salesman followed her, holding the red boots aloft and murmuring his regrets; "To have such an elegant customer leave without purchasing boots that suited her so perfectly was a great shame!"

Janine got out on the first floor near lady's cosmetics, and wondered how Parisian women could spend so much of their time shopping. It was not a task she enjoyed. Even though she regretted that she couldn't afford the red boots. It had been worth leaving them behind to get a line on the Princess. Since the Ritz wasn't too far out of the way, and it was still early, she decided to hop on the subway to get there faster. She would take a chance that someone had noticed something odd about Saroya's unexpected departure from that pricey, historic hotel.

The Ritz was located in one of the most elegant quarters of Paris. It was a fine old hotel with a checkered past. Herman Goering had stayed there during the German occupation of Paris, using it as a convenient rest house near the Louvre and the Orangerie. His mission was to collect paintings for the Third Reich and, not incidentally, a selection for his own private collection of old masters. But the hotel had outlived that and a number of other scandals. Like a great actress who has known glory in her past, she still presented an elegant face to the public. Her public rooms were filled with some priceless original furniture.

Though the hotel's clients were somewhat more casual than had been the case in earlier days, Janine still felt a bit underdressed. The lobby crowd this morning consisted of businessmen in elegantly cut suits and a few Arabs wearing the traditional white robes and red-checkered headdress of the Saudi aristocracy. Janine was taller than some of the Arab men, but they still cast appraising glances in her direction as she strode by. She looked straight ahead, intent on business, as she moved to the front desk, hoping to find a chatty clerk. She was quickly disappointed. The one elegantly dressed clerk was busy with the telephone and checking people out of the hotel. He barely glanced in her direction.

Janine decided to try the concierge desk. There was a sandy haired, smartly dressed young man seated behind the desk, looking somewhat uncomfortable. She surmised that it might not be his regular position. She was right. Her inquiries about which tours left the hotel and when, were answered with his sideways glance. Janine repeated her question in English, though her French was excellent. " I am very sorry," the young man replied. " If you can wait a few minutes

Monsieur Henri will return. I am just taking his place for a few moments while he looks after some important guests."

"Then you think that my wishes are not important?" Janine answered casually, in her unaccented French.

The young man almost jumped out of his chair. He was so used to dealing with Americans who neither understood his language, or mangled it when they tried to speak it that he couldn't cover his embarrassment. "What does Madame wish to see, in our beautiful city?" he asked, regaining his composure quickly. A credit to his hotel training.

"I would like to take the tours that Princess Saroya took," Janine said, sitting down and taking a chance on dropping the name.

The young man looked blank. He ran a hand through his sandy hair, upsetting its carefully tousled look. "The Saudi aristocracy does not usually take tours, Madame," he answered politely, as if speaking to a retarded child. "They have their own chauffeured limousines when they leave the hotel. Indeed. I never saw the Princess leave except in a limousine provided by her country, with her own private driver."

Bingo! Janine smiled in satisfaction. He had seen her leave. She now had to proceed carefully for fear of scaring him off. " How silly of me," she said, reaching for her handbag. "How much is the tour of the Louvre and when does it leave?"

The young man handed her several brochures. There were a number of companies providing specialized tours of all of the points of interest in Paris, the Louvre among them. Janine shuffled the brochures, and then stood up to leave as though undecided. She turned back abruptly. "When the Princess left was her brother, Said, with her?"

The young man looked startled. "I would not know, Madame. She was with two Saudi gentlemen dressed in black suits. She left unexpectedly, I was told." And then he blushed, as though he had uttered something indiscreet. Which indeed he had.

Janine sat down again. Now that she had him talking she was going to milk everything out of him that she could. But they were interrupted by his supervisor, the senior concierge, who carried with him all the elegance and savoir-faire of the Ritz reputation.

Janine picked up her fan of brochures and hastily retreated in the direction of the famous Hemingway Bar, to regroup and think about what she had learned so far. She wasn't aware that one of the men in the lobby excused himself from the group he was engaged with and followed her silently into the bar.

The bar was dark and deserted at this hour of the morning. Janine seated herself at a corner table in a gilded Louis the Sixteenth chair, and thought about her options. Ordering a drink was not one of them, as the bartender was absent. She shuffled the brochures and tried to look as though she was considering a tour. A hand grabbed her shoulder, and put pressure on it so that she couldn't move or turn around. Then a low voice behind her spoke rapidly in heavily accented French. "You will stop looking for our little sister," the voice said, pushing her hard against the back of the chair. "She has disgraced her brother, by her actions. And he will take care of her to preserve the honor of the family."

Janine felt as though she had been punched in the belly. She knew how Saroya would be taken care of by her family. Death for dishonor was the family code, neither Janine, her agency, nor the Paris police, could do anything to prevent it, even if they tried.

Chapter Seven

Janine knew that she had been given two impossible assignments. If Saroya was in the hands of her family, and they were determined to punish her by death, or a number of other banishments that might be worse than death for a young woman who had tasted a short period of freedom in Paris. Janine had been warned in no uncertain terms to stay away from the case. And she doubted if even her bosses in the agency would want her to pursue this any further. But she was wrong. When she repeated the incident in the Hemingway Bar on the telephone, her boss was adamant. "We've been asked by the Saudi King to look into this matter as a personal favor. Our president has requested that we pursue the matter. Have you gotten to be such a sissy that some unknown bozo threatening you in a bar, scares you off the case?"

Janine wanted to tell him in no uncertain terms where he could stick his case. But some part of her felt a real sympathy for the Princess. At the moment she didn't have a clue what to do about it, or how to proceed. But she assured her boss that she would keep looking into it, but with a little more tact. She didn't want Saroya killed just because she had probably had a date with someone her brother disapproved of. She might even have slept with him. That was a crime punishable by death in the eyes of the more orthodox Moslems, particularly of the Saudi persuasion.

Janine left the hotel and hopped on a crowded subway to take her to the area where Jalila Haddad was supposed to be speaking. The French Algerian woman was a newly appointed minister, given the responsibility of trying to improve housing in the turbulent suburbs, where thousands of unemployed young people still lived with their families in overcrowded public housing. These 'bergs', as they were called, were a recipe for despair and a breeding ground for all kinds of violence and a kindergarten for terrorists.

Janine climbed out of the subway and faced a world that was one hundred degrees different from the opulent hotel she had just left. She was surrounded by tall pock- marked buildings that spoke of despair. Their only decoration was graffiti that covered the buildings as high as a

Anne Kimbell

person could reach. The slogans were full of hate for the government, the housing authority, the police and some other phrases in Arabic that Janine thankfully couldn't translate. She made her way quickly to the public hall where today's meeting was to be held. The scrutinizing looks that she got were not too unfriendly, mostly curious, as though wondering what a decently dressed woman was doing in this neighborhood, at this time of day, without children tagging along behind her, clutching at her skirt.

The auditorium was crowded and smelled of unwashed bodies pressed too closely together. There were more women than men. Most of the women were wearing headscarves and holding small children by the hand or in their arms. A fat Frenchman dressed in a rumpled black suit introduced the newly appointed Minister of Housing and Welfare. He wiped his face with a handkerchief before he began to speak, looking as though he would rather be anywhere than here. The crowd mumbled and surged back and forth, hardly paying attention to him. But all that changed when Jalila Haddad took the stage.

She was a thin young woman with cropped black hair, a pinched looking face with dark eyes and thin eyebrows. She wore a gray suit and white blouse that showed the signs of repeated launderings. She gazed out over the crowd for a few moments, utterly silent, watching them. Slowly the audience began to quiet down. Then she began to speak. Her voice was low and vibrant. As she talked, her slender body almost vibrated as though it was an instrument that she was playing. She told the crowd that she was one of them. She had grown up in this very neighborhood. Suffered the indignities that living here had heaped upon them all; the bad or non existent schools, the crime, the disgust of other French citizens who considered them all second class because their parents and grandparents had migrated from Algeria, in search of a better life.

"But what did we get?" she asked the audience. "To live here like animals in a cage. To see our daughters raped and dishonored, so that no good man would have them in marriage. To have no social services to care for our sick, our elderly." She paused dramatically, her lips pressed together and her hands clenched at her sides as though to keep from screaming. "But I promise you that will change. Or I will die trying to change it. If you will help me, we can make a better life!"

Now the crowd was silent, as though holding its collective breath. Then it exploded in a roar, calling her name over and over again, "Jelila, Jelila, Jelila." She was one of theirs and she was promising to help them. Janine stood back, shaking her head. She had seen crowds like this before, seen them turn to rip the speaker apart, but the young woman seemed totally unafraid. This was her place, this was her mission and she was going to accomplish it or give her life and her honor for it.

Janine wanted to meet her. But the crowd of well-wishers was too thick to even approach her. Janine lingered at the outskirts of the crowd, hoping that it would thin enough for her to have a word with the young woman. But now several men who looked like security guards were hurrying Haddad out of the building. Janine followed and saw her escorted into a waiting SUV with a government decal on the side. She took note of the agency. Perhaps a telephone call would get her an appointment. She wanted to meet the young woman for more than business reasons. Everything that she had said had resonated with Janine. The woman was a fighter and Janine respected her for that. Even though looking around the neighborhood, it seemed as though she was tackling overwhelming odds. But if there was a center of discontent and a breeding ground for Jihadists in Paris, this was certainly the middle of it.

Chapter Eight

Rick had been ringing Janine's phone off and on all morning, but she didn't pick up. He wasn't sure if she was ignoring him or if for some reason she had turned off her cell. He finally got through to her with his news. There had been a huge explosion at his company's work site in Algiers. A number of workers had been injured, among them the American contractors who were supervising the site. That had sent a wave of concern through the company. They were loath to lose the contract with the Algerian government, but they weren't at all sure that the security they had been promised was enough.

"We can't expect our contractors to work fully armed. Besides this was a bomb. Planted in one of the pipes along the construction site, and it was a type only made in France. That's the kicker."

"So you want to know what I have found out, if anything." Janine said acerbically. "Well, for your information, I have been mostly taken off the case to look for a missing Saudi princess."

Rick almost laughed, "Not Saroya, I hope. She has broken every rule of Saudi propriety and then some. I'm surprised that she is still alive."

"I'm not certain that she is," Janine answered grimly. "But what do you expect me to do about your explosion?"

"Just wondered if you had heard anything? I probably have to fly to Algiers in the next couple of days. Wondered if you had any leads."

"Nada." Janine answered bluntly. "I'm fishing in an empty barrel."

"Then since we are both in the same boat. Would you like to have dinner?"

Janine was taken aback by his unusually friendly tone, and his offer. Whatever his ulterior motives, she did have to eat. And she was curious about what had happened in Algiers. It hadn't yet made the newspapers or CNN. But these incidents were becoming so common that they no longer made immediate headlines. Clearly Rick was worried, and she was at a loss, so why not have dinner with him? What could she lose?

They met in a small Moroccan restaurant on the Blvd St. Germain, not far from Janine's apartment. Janine knew the proprietor and that the cous cous and tangine were authentic and excellent. She had maintained a taste for this healthy food from Tunisia and she knew that Rick liked it too. She had surprised herself by dressing carefully for the occasion, as though it were a date. But the slim black skirt and silk blouse made her feel competent and pretty, even though it wasn't a date in the real sense of the word. She and Rick knew each other too well for that. There was too much bad history between them.

Rick, when he arrived, ten minutes late as usual, was in jeans and a black turtle neck shirt with a herringbone jacket. His hair was grayer at the temples, but he was still a good-looking man, if a little rough around the edges. He was clearly on edge. He apologized for being late as he sat down, glancing around him to check out the other diners. They were early, so they were almost alone in the restaurant. He seemed relieved.

The proprietor greeted them warmly and then left them with menus, and a couple of suggestions about the evening's specials. Rick glanced at the menu and then asked Janine to order for them. He was too on edge to think about food. There had been another explosion on the work site this afternoon, more people were injured, several very seriously. "The insurgents are trying to shut us down," he said grimly. "There is no way that we can check every pipe on the construction site. The bastards know that. But this is their own water purification project that they are murdering. This means fresh water for thousands of families along the river. The end of pollution that has gone on for generations."

" How do you know for sure that it's Algerians?" Janine asked, dipping warm, flat bread into the garlic-seasoned bowl of humus in the center of the table.

Rick glared at her in frustration. "It could be anybody. Paid thugs, Jihadists. But there is no way that we can quickly secure a work site that covers a dozen acres. We have to find the source and quickly."

The portly owner brought a huge plate of steaming cous cous covered with chicken and vegetables and placed it proudly in the center of the table. The aroma spoke of Tunisia and the many meals that they had eaten together there. For a moment neither of them spoke, remembering. Then Janine served her plate and offered to do the same for Rick. He nodded assent, gratefully. Maybe food would calm the gnawing in his stomach that he had been fighting with all day. This was supposed to be his last big assignment. A chance to go out in glory. It looked as though it was turning into a nightmare, with no ending except a bomb going off.

Janine spoke thoughtfully. "The one clean clue you have is that the bomb components were French. That doesn't really prove anything except it wasn't a home made job like the roadside bombs used in Iraq and Afghanistan. Is there any reason why the French would be against an American company taking on this assignment, and perhaps giving the insurgents a push in your company's direction?"

Rick shook his head, dipping into his fragrant cous cous. He found that he was suddenly starving. "French companies have the lion's share of the construction of new buildings and the huge shopping center. The water purification project is just a minor part of the whole gizmo. Why would they want to help sabotage it? It doesn't make sense."

"But it's an integral part. Without cleaning up the port, how attractive will the rest of the area be? Isn't there a marina planned? And there has to be clean water for all the people who live in those newly constructed apartments. Sounds as though your company has a vital piece. Killing your particular part might have a domino effect on the whole project."

Rick nodded. As usual Janine was thinking outside the box. That's why he had to convince her to come to Algiers with him. But he hadn't a clue as to how he was going to finesse it.

****

The young Arab, parked outside the restaurant in a battered *deux chevaux*, had been waiting patiently for over an hour, watching Janine and her friend eat their dinner at a table near the front window. His orders had been only to watch her and report back. But his fingers itched to pull the knife that he carried hidden under his coat. It was a sharp knife and it would go cleanly into her throat. One more infidel sent to wherever they went. Certainly not to paradise. He shifted in his seat. This watching was boring. Not what he had expected to do. He wanted action. He wanted to spill blood. But all that he was allowed to do was to watch and report back. A baby could do this, a child. And he was no longer a child. He was a trained Jahadist ready and willing to die for Allah.

Now the infidels were leaving the restaurant. He took a chance and left the car parked illegally to follow them down the street. The woman was talking and laughing, looking up at the man. How shameless these women were. Showing themselves on the street with their hair hanging loose and looking into men's eyes to tempt them into carnal desire. Women were all the same; they were the tempters of men. This one especially. He could feel the knife burning against his belly, begging him for her blood.

Someone caught him roughly by the shoulder. He turned, reaching for his knife, ready to strike. But it was just an old man, the owner of the restaurant. Telling him not to leave his car parked illegally or he would call the police. The man spoke in Arabic, in a firm tone. He walked the young man back to his car and stood there until he moved it. The jihadist turned, his quarry, the woman, was gone. He could see the couple walking down the street together. Now the man was talking to the woman earnestly, as though he was trying to convince her of something. The young man touched the knife inside his worn coat. Soon it would taste blood. Soon he would have this silver haired woman begging for his mercy. But he had no mercy. Not for the temptress.

Chapter Nine

Rick left Janine at her door with a brief "Good night" and "think about Algiers". Hardly the ending of a romantic date. That was what it once had been. Too much time had passed since their affair in Tunisia, and neither of them were the same people. 'Thank goodness,' Janine sighed as she climbed the stairs to her apartment. Rick's invitation to go to Algiers was tempting, if only to get a better line on what she was looking for in Paris. Or maybe it would just be a chance to get away from the problem for a few days and find a better perspective.

She really didn't know exactly what she was looking for here in Paris. The task of searching for Saroya seemed to be a dead end. Whatever had happened to her, her brother was certainly behind it, and she had no desire to tangle in any way with the Saudi royal family. Rumor had it that their vengeance against infidels, especially female ones, was swift and terrible. Janine didn't fancy getting her throat cut. Not at this point in her career. She would have shuddered if she had guessed how close she had come to having it slit this evening.

She also would not have slept so soundly if she had known that just downstairs, inside the foyer, a young man slumped, nursing his frustration and anger. He had missed the infidel tonight. But she would soon feel the cold steel of his knife. He only had to wait a little longer until the street and building were quiet, then he would strike. He could wait patiently; Allah gave him patience, which was as strong as his faith. He felt his cell phone vibrate against his hip. He ignored it as he imagined what he would do to the woman. It vibrated again, longer, whoever it was would not give up. He held it to his ear and pressed 'answer'. The voice on the other end was stern. "Your mission is cancelled for tonight. Return to us, we have more important things for you to do, for the brotherhood." He slipped quietly out of the foyer, hiding his knife and closing the door behind him softly. Janine slept on. But it was a troubled sleep, filled with strange images of danger, and of being followed by men in white robes, through a dark and shuttered Arab marketplace.

****

Rick hardly slept at all. He had to find some way to get Janine to come with him to Algeria. He knew that she was reluctant to leave Paris at this time, even if her bosses would permit it. But he had a strong hunch that with her help he might find the source of the trouble in Algiers. He had to figure out a way to make this trip as important to her as it was to him. Not for any personal reasons, he assured himself. This was purely business. "Yeah, right," he muttered, as he got up at two a.m. to take a drink of seltzer water. The cous cous had settled into a hard lump in the middle of his gut. He swilled down the fizzing water and then sat down in a chair to think.

What would entice her to come with him? It wasn't his sexual charm. She had made it pretty clear that whatever had ever been between them was totally over and done with. He had felt that way too, until he had seen her again. There was something about her, her 'take no prisoners' attitude that made her fascinating to men. Himself included. Perhaps it was her air of not needing anybody for long, which he suspected was true, that made men want to be the one to change her mind and have her come crawling back begging for more.

He laughed at the fantasy of Janine crawling, begging for someone to care about her. He rubbed his aching eyes, turned out the light, and tried unsuccessfully to fall back asleep. But sleep would not come. He kept running over various scenarios to get Janine to commit to Algiers. About four a.m., he finally hit on the perfect bait. Then he fell soundly asleep.

The next morning he awoke with the question still in his mind, but he realized that he had forgotten the answer that had come to him so clearly in the middle of the night. So much for not writing his great ideas down when they kept him awake. He was berating himself mentally, over a strong cup of French coffee, when he got his answer via the morning edition of *Le Monde*. The newspaper announced, on an inside page, that the new Minister of Housing and Welfare, Jalila Haddad, was going to Algiers to visit the developing sites for urban renewal and low cost housing. The major development mentioned was the one where his company was involved in purifying the water supply. He wondered if Janine had seen the article. Haddad's trip to Algiers was the perfect bait to get her to accompany him. The article mentioned that security would be tight, given the number of the recent bombings attributed to al Qaida.

The *Le Monde* article surmised that the Minister would be a high value target, given her public denouncements of the Algerian unrest. She was now 'a third generation French citizen', she had said proudly and was opposed to continuing a war that had brought so much misery and destruction to her people. She would go to Algiers only to learn what she could to help other homeless people in France. She dared the Jahidists to disrupt her trip. Rick shook his head in disbelief. The lady was either pretty sure of herself, or setting herself up as a target for some reason known only to herself.

He called Janine after his third cup of coffee, not to seem too eager.

She was just leaving to check in at the office. And 'yes' she had seen the newspaper article, and she was as surprised as Rick was. "Sounds as if she is daring them to attack her," she said, cradling her cell phone under her chin as she locked the apartment and started down the stairs, two steps at a time.

"You'll never get a better chance to check out Algerian sources for al Qaida. Sure that you don't want to come?"

"I'll check with the boss this morning," Janine answered hurriedly. She knew that he was right. And she had a vested interest in seeing that Haddad came to no harm. She liked the sincerity of the young woman, even though her statements made it sound as though she was inviting trouble. Trouble that Janine knew the dissidents would be only to happy to provide in their home territory. It made no difference to them that Haddad was third generation Algerian. By her own statements, she was now French, and a member of the hated French government as well.

What a great feather in their caps to take her out publicly. What a show of their power in France that would be. Janine knew that they had ways of getting through even the most carefully managed security. And on construction sites, Haddad would be an easy target.

The question was, would her boss approve the trip on such flimsy grounds. She was supposed to be still looking for Saroya and there was no way that she could tie this trip to the missing Saudi Princess, who had probably already been flown home in disgrace on a private jet. Unless her brother, despite his loud protests to the contrary, had already decided to do away with her to preserve the family honor. Such deaths were done routinely in the Kingdom. Women being of relatively minor value, even royal ones.

Janine again took a bus to her office near the American Embassy, but located just far enough away to be discrete. When she got there, the 'boys' were in a meeting. Her sandy haired boss greeted her casually, and waved her to a seat at the far end of the table. She noticed that he was beginning to get a slight paunch and that his jacket could barely button over his dark blue trousers. Too much good French food she imagined, at his daily gourmet lunches that included several glasses of wine. But he was still sharp. He had survived all the current changes of direction the agency had recently taken. He had a good enough record and enough friends in high places to keep this plum job, despite the twists and turns of the present administration. The president seemed to believe that, when all else failed, he could always blame his wrong turns on the CIA, as long as they were willing to roll over and take the blame.

Janine said little. She didn't have much to report on her current dual assignments. So she sat quietly in the 'clean' room and listened to her colleagues make their reports. Much was said and little was known as far as she could ascertain. The new French government had given them a lot to speculate about but not too much real information. The problem of al Qaida in France, and in the other countries surrounding the Mediterranean, was on everyone's minds. Each officer had a piece of the puzzle, but so far nothing concrete. Janine made her report at the very end. She had very little to report on the missing Saudi princess, but an interesting turn of affairs vis a vis the new French/Algerian Minister of Housing and Welfare, who was traveling to Algiers sometime in the next week.

She mentioned casually that it might be worth following her to see what leads she could pick up. Her boss looked at her quizzically, and then glanced around the table at the other officers.

There seemed to be a kind of telepathy going on among the group of men. Janine definitely was not on their wavelength. But she thought that she could read their minds. Why not get her out of Paris for a few days. If she botched the job, it would be on her head. And if she uncovered something of value it could only make the office look good. So why not send her?

Her boss nodded at her as he stood up. "Get personnel to cut a travel requisition for a few days for you. I assume that you don't have to stay at the Algerian equivalent of the Ritz, if there is such a thing."

"I doubt it" Janine answered, quelling the childish desire to kick him in the shins. Instead she smiled around the table at her co-workers. "See you in a few days," she said brightly. "Don't catch all the terrorists while I'm gone."

She strode out of the office with the wind whipping her short hair and a great sense of relief. Much to her surprise, she was looking forward to getting out of Paris. And even spending some time with Rick didn't seem like such a bad idea. She liked what she had seen of Haddad. The idea of providing some covert protection for her appealed to her sense of sisterhood. Not that she would have much of a chance to interact with the Minister. But even being around the fringes of the visit, especially with the introduction that Rick provided to his project, might give her some help with her current assignment to identify some of the French/Algerian Jihadists. Luck might just be with her on this trip.

The morning was turning cool, with one of those sudden changes of temperature that Paris was famous for. She walked through the Tuilerie Gardens with the wind scattering what was left of the colorful autumn leaves around her feet. There were a few young children playing discreetly in the pathways with their ever-watchful nannies on the alert. Janine caught a ball and rolled it back to a solemn looking little boy about five. He smiled shyly and said '*merci*,' as his nanny nodded at him approvingly. Janine appreciated his manners and the smile that he gave her. She sometimes wished that life could always be this uncomplicated. She shuddered and pulled her jacket more tightly around her, as the chilling wind whirled around her.

She needed to let Rick know that she was cleared to go to Algiers, as soon as she could get a visa. Not too easy a task for an American at this moment in time. Especially one with an official passport. If Rick wanted her to go badly enough, perhaps he could get a letter from his company requesting her services as a 'consultant.' They might as well get the same plane if possible. It would make transportation from the airport simpler. It would insert her more easily into the situation if she came as his assistant, or whatever cover Rick's company could provide for her. That was his call. Thinking about calling, she got him on his cell and gave him the news that she had been cleared to go. "Can your company give me a reason to visit the site and look as if I belong there?"

Rick responded with a smile in his voice. "I will personally give you a tour and provide you with a hard hat. What do you know about water purification?"

"Not much, but I'm a quick study."

" Then I'll introduce you as a consultant."

"Sounds good, Bring the specs and I can learn enough on the plane to sound intelligent. How soon are you leaving?"

" I need to get out in the next few days. Can you pull some strings to get a quick business visa?"

"Probably, based on a letter from your company saying that I am essential to your project."

"It's as good a done. I have a drawer full of letterhead."

"Fax me a letter as soon as you can. I'll drop it at personnel and let them take care of the details. Some of the beleaguered ladies there are on my side." She smiled into the phone. "The 'boys' don't treat them any better than they treat me and that makes for comradeship on the lower levels."

Janine strolled along the Seine on her way home, thinking about Algeria. She hadn't been there since before she served in Tunisia. It had been a grim city then, years after the French had all departed. Tall apartment buildings, deserted by the French settlers, had been inhabited by Arab squatters from the desert. There had been a lack of electricity on the main streets and the ancient Casbah was totally off limits for tourists. She knew that the city had changed a lot in recent years, with the election of a more moderate president who was doing all that he could to bring Algeria into the modern world. But the current terrorist attacks were a setback, as were the statistics on French tourists who had been ambushed and murdered in recent years. It wasn't exactly a place one would choose at the moment for a restful vacation.

But Janine was always exhilarated by change, and a new challenge. Rick's company gave her the perfect excuse to visit the city again. She was curious about the project that they were developing. The fact that it had become a target for attack was interesting information. Was it because it was an American company? Or were the jihadists just against anything that looked like progress? Keeping the country in disarray was a good way to increase their power. If no one could guess where the next attack was coming from, that kept the police, the army and all the other security forces off base and unable to act coherently. That is what terrorists always did, find an unprotected spot and go for it.

She saw young people strolling hand and hand along the riverbank, despite the cold wind. The booksellers were beginning to cover their wares with plastic. She nodded at several that she recognized from her strolls. On an impulse she stopped at one 'bookanist' who sold maps, both old and new. She asked for one of Algeria, and found that he had several. One was a slightly used tourist map with camels imposed over images of the Sahara and enticing photographs of the Roman ruins at Djemila and Timgad along the coast.

She had seen those years ago on her first trip from Tunisia and wondered if they were still as virtually untouched as they had been at that time. Another older map showed the winding streets of the Casbah. The ancient original town that was now, as it had always been, a place of 'tourists beware.' Not only of pickpockets, but also of the danger of getting your throat slit in a dark street. She bought both maps. One for general information and the other one for sentimental reasons.

The bookseller smiled at her as she bargained amicably for the maps and finally gave her a small discount since she was purchasing two. He wrapped them in brown paper and Janine shoved them into her handbag. Once she had a map she always felt half way to her new destination. She realized that she had been feeling a bit stuck and on the shelf in Paris. The challenge of Algeria made her stride longer. She approached Rue Belle Chasse with her chin out and her face to the wind.

Chapter Ten

A week later, Janine was seated on an Air France flight to Algiers in first class, courtesy of Rick's company. Her agency would never have paid the extra 500 dollars, but Rick seemed delighted to do so to get her there in style. She also had a letter in her bag, signed by the president of his company, giving her a limited assignment as a water purification consultant, amount of salary to be decided by Rick Harrison. Janine smiled and tucked it back in her briefcase along with her hard won visa from the Algerian Embassy in Paris. It had taken a copy of the work assignment letter to convince them that she wasn't going there to spy on their government.

She had spent the week trying in vain to track down some clue as to what had happened to Princess Saroya. Every avenue seemed closed and every inquiry, even a discreet one to a good contact at the Saudi Embassy had come up with nothing. It was as if the woman had vanished off the face of the earth. Even her numerous maids had disappeared. Her Saudi contact had implied that perhaps her brother was 'punishing her at home,' in his palace. Janine had heard stories of Saudi women, accused of giving their sexual favors to infidels, being locked indefinitely in a padded room with no windows and only a slot for food, until they either died or went mad. She found such a medieval custom hard to believe. It ranked along with the chastity belt women were locked into during the crusades. But in Saudi Arabia there wasn't the possibility of becoming a nun and spending the rest of your days atoning for you sins by doing good works. The men in that country made sure that you repented long and painfully.

She sighed and stretched out her long legs. First class wasn't bad. She liked the leather seats and the constant attention of the flight attendants, even though it wasn't too long a flight. She had left early to get to Algiers before the end of the day. Rick had given her a lengthy prospectus to study on his water purification project. It was indeed unique for the Arab world and for anywhere else for that matter. His company intended to install huge filters and turbines on the floor of the river that would act not only to purify the water but also to generate much needed electricity. It was a revolutionary concept, labor intensive and very costly. Something similar had been tried in the East River in New York and was still bogged down in permits and funding. That was one reason that this project was so important and such a source of pride for the Algerians. When this was completed, it would be a model for industrialized society trying to clean up their own rivers and return them to their natural state.

If the project was ever completed, and that was a big 'If.' It was clear from the recent attacks on the site that someone or some group was eager to see that it was never finished. The delays in construction due to the bombings, and loss of personnel, were making the project daily more costly. It was harder and harder to get trained people to stay on the job. And any one of the hundreds of semi-skilled Algerian workmen could be one of the jihadists. She accepted a tray with a salad and soft drink from the dark eyed hostess, who greeted her in French and asked politely if she would need anything else. Janine ordered a coffee for later and tucked into the excellent seafood salad with gusto. This was much better than eating a sandwich in the back of the plane, even if it was served on a crusty baguette.

She must have drifted off to sleep, because as she awoke, the captain was asking his passengers to fasten their seat belts. They would be landing in Algiers in fifteen minutes. The approach was bumpy and Janine, even though she was accustomed to flying, held on tightly to the arm rests as they circled the city. Through the window Janine could see what looked, from the air, like a modern city set on the edge of a turquoise sea. Flat roofed suburbs stretched out toward the Atlas Mountains, which were still covered with green. She knew that the French had grown all manner of fruit trees on these slopes and wondered if after all these years any of them were still bearing fruit. No wonder that the French had been so loathe to leave. The land along the coast was extremely fertile and in many ways reminded them of the South of France.

The plane jolted to a stop, lifted for one hair-raising moment by a gust of wind off the Mediterranean. Janine unbuckled her seat belt and reached for her brief case and carry on bag. She hadn't been willing to submit her laptop and few items of essential clothing to the vagaries of luggage handlers.

A dark haired Arab man, wearing a cream colored linen suit, who had been eyeing her during the flight, reached up and lifted down her laptop and carry on before she could do it herself. "Are you new to our country, is this your first visit, Madame?" he asked in slightly accented French. "Please allow me to assist you in finding transportation to your hotel."

Janine thanked him and accepted his help in lifting down her belongings. He smelled of lime aftershave and was well groomed even after the flight. Janine felt somewhat rumpled and groggy after her nap. She smoothed out her light-weight pantsuit and tied a scarf around her hair, thanking the man for his help. "It is nothing," he answered graciously. "It is always my privilege to help visitors to my country. I have a car waiting and would be happy to drop you at your hotel."

"That is very kind," Janine answered, matching his gracious tone. "But I expect that I am being met."

"Are you here on business?" the man continued, following her closely down the aisle.

Janine was trapped behind the slow moving couple in front of her, who were having trouble getting their travel cases out of the overhead rack. She didn't intend to answer, but she could literally feel the man breathing down her neck, waiting for a reply.

"I am here on pleasure," she lied, for no reason except that she was annoyed at the man's insistence.

"Ah, pleasure is something that I know a great deal about," he breathed in her ear. "Perhaps you will let me help you experience it in my city." As the couple in front of them finally began to move forward, he handed Janine his card. "My home is an old palace in the Casbah, perhaps you would enjoy seeing it one afternoon."

Janine nodded briskly, for once without a reply. She hoped that Rick would be there to meet her or at least had sent a company car. This man's attention unnerved her a bit. He was standing so close that she could feel the heat of his body through her lightweight clothing. She had the strong feeling that his interest was more than personal. But she gave him a slight smile and nodded her head as she tucked his card into the side of her briefcase. "Thank you for you kind offer," she said crisply. "I will keep it in mind."

The air was warm, but a breeze from the Mediterranean was keeping the day from being stifling. She moved quickly through customs. Fortunately the man from the plane was in the residents' line so she didn't see him again until she was out of the airport, looking for Rick or for some other means of transportation to her hotel. She had chosen the Hilton, since it was close to the project and frequented by many Americans. She assumed that Rick was staying there too, since he had recommended it. There was no sign of him or of a vehicle bearing the name of the hotel. A few taxies stood patiently in line while their drivers eyed her boldly. Several approached her, trying to usher her into their cars with promises of cheap fares and a quick ride.

She resisted. She still hoped that Rick would appear. She had a number of questions about the project that she wanted answers to as soon as possible. She saw the man from the plane emerge from the terminal with several large and expensive looking suitcases. 'Probably Parisian dresses for his wife or girlfriends,' Janine reflected, somewhat amused. He waved down a waiting black limousine. The driver was helping him to store his luggage, when he again caught sight of Janine and gestured toward his transportation. Janine waved back and shook her head. She preferred one of the taxi drivers to his unwanted attentions in a limo.

Rick arrived in the nick of time. He came wheeling up in a battered jeep with the company's initials on the side. He jumped out of the car and greeted Janine warmly. She gave him an unexpected hug, which floored him. "I'm getting rid of some unwanted curiosity from a man I met on the plane. Don't take it personally," she hissed in his ear.

He grinned and hugged her back. His body felt strong and familiar under his thin cotton shirt. He was wearing shorts and desert boots and a hard hat, and he was somewhat grimy. "Sorry to be late to meet you," he said eyeing the black limo as is slid past them.

" Looks like you passed up a great chance to get introduced to high society in Algiers."

"Do you know that man?" Janine asked as she climbed into the jeep beside him.

"Let's say I know his type. He probably has fingers in a dozen pies, most of them slightly illegal and some of them rampantly so. This society is in such flux that it is easy for a man like him to make a buck or two, smuggling oil, arms, cocaine, even women to anyone who can pay his price. It gives him a lifestyle that he couldn't afford anywhere else on the planet."

"Well, then I'm glad that I didn't take him up on his invitation to visit him in the Casbah."

Rick shrugged. "You probably could have fought your way out. But after drinking one of his drugged cocktails, you might not have wanted to."

"Gee! Think what I've just been saved from," Janine, grinned, securing her scarf around her wildly blowing hair. "Sold into a life of sin at my age."

Rick glanced over at her wryly. "Most of his clients want women about thirteen. So you are a bit long in the tooth for that duty. Maybe he just wanted to know what you were up to in visiting Algiers. We don't get many single women visitors right now."

"And exactly what am I up to? Have you picked up any leads?"

Rick shook his head. "Let's get back to the hotel first. There are several possibilities I would like to run by you."

"When does Minister Haddad arrive?"

"Day after tomorrow."

"What are the local security preparations for her visit?"

"As far as we can tell, not nearly enough for her viewing of our site. That's where you come in," he said quietly, as he dropped her off in front of the hotel. "I'll fill you in over dinner, after I have a chance to wash off most of the Sahara, and put on a clean shirt."

Janine handed her laptop and carry on to a smiling porter and strode inside to register. The hotel's air conditioning hit her like a blast from a refrigerator. She pulled off her scarf and walked up to an elegant front desk that was deserted except for one sleepy looking clerk, who greeted her in heavily accented English. 'Yes, her room was ready; she would be taken to it right away.' Then he added politely, "Would Madame mind waiting for a moment for someone to escort her to her room?"

Janine thanked him but took her key and instructions to finding her room. She didn't have enough luggage to warrant an escort, and she was longing for a cool shower and a chance to continue to look over the information that Rick had just given her. Her long nap on the plane had eaten up most of her study time. She wanted to be up to speed by dinnertime, and ready to really quiz him carefully about his company's arrangements for the Minister's visit to his site.

Her room was high up in the hotel with a breathtaking view of the bay. From this altitude, it was almost like being in a plane. The poverty below was obscured by her birds' eye view of the city below. She took out her map of Algiers and oriented herself. That was something that she had learned from her military father. Always know exactly where you are at all times and what the escape routes were. She had checked the stairwells on her way up, after the elevator ride. She knew that there were two on each floor and where they led. Now she had to do the same thing with the construction site if possible, and also the Casbah. Which she did intend to visit, even though it was now considered off limits and too dangerous for tourists. Her meeting with

Amir on the plane, for that was the name on his heavily embossed card, had piqued her interest. He was probably involved in exactly the type of activities that she had come to investigate. She was a big girl and she was used to taking care of herself in the Arab world.

****

After dinner with Rick in a quiet café that served excellent French and Algerian food, she had a lot more to think about. The insurgents in Algeria were claiming that they had attacked Tunisian border guards in the south of the country just a few days ago. Five guards had been killed. The Tunisians were calling it a 'border crossing accident,' denying that militants were in any way involved. But Rick's take on the 'accident,' was that the militants were getting more and more self confident, taking risks to try to extend their reach into Tunisia, which had defiantly resisted the election of an Islamic party to power in the last decade.

"This means that they are out to show their strength, and what better way than attacking a French Minister of Algerian decent, who just happens to be a woman."

"And who will probably be walking around a construction site her with her face uncovered for all the Arab workmen to see."

Rick nodded. " Except that she won't be walking, she will be riding. And if you agree, you will be riding shotgun beside her."

"Why me?" Janine asked taken aback, but only for a moment.

"Because you now work for our company. temporarily. But more important because you are a woman and the insurgents will be more apt to show themselves if she is only accompanied by another woman."

"You mean that you hired me as bait."

"Something like that."

"But your backup will be right behind us, I assume."

"In the car behind and in front and on both sides, if possible."

"Sounds like a panzer movement."

"Are you up for it?" He grinned, daring her to say 'no.'

Janine toyed with her skewered shrimp for a minute. Then she looked up at him and nodded calmly. "I like the lady and I sure don't want to see her kidnapped or killed, which is probably what the bad guys have in mind." She wiped her mouth delicately with her napkin. "So count me in, but make darn sure that we are covered from all sides."

Rick looked over at her, his eyes cold. "I will be there lady, right behind you. You can be sure of that." Seeing her wary expression he continued. "You're a valuable asset to the company; we don't want you dead or kidnapped before we get our money's worth."

Janine looked shocked, then she grinned: "Rick that is the nicest thing that anyone has said to me recently. I will do my job and I promise that you won't need to rescue either of us from the bad guys. My reputation depends on it."

Chapter Eleven

Janine had been wondering about how to arrange a visit to the Casbah. She had spent the morning with Rick going over security plans for the Minister's visit, and inspecting the enormous work site for opportunities for the insurgents to attack. There were so many possibilities that it made her head swim. She finally concurred with the Algerian government's estimate that if would be best if the Minister didn't come to the site at all. But if she had to come, her visit should be limited to the offices and going up on one heavily guarded platform from where she could observe most of the ongoing operation. Taking her on a real tour would be virtually impossible, if they were going to protect her safety on this official visit.

With those decisions made and plans in place, Janine had the afternoon to herself. The Minister wasn't expected to arrive until afternoon of the next day. Janine went to her room and tried to read but she was restless. From one of her windows, she could just see a corner of the ancient Casbah spilling white and gray buildings down an adjacent hill. She had inquired casually at the hotel desk for a guide, but was told in no uncertain terms that it was a 'treacherous place' not worth a visit. Janine correctly surmised that the government was not encouraging tourists to go there at all.

A magazine in her room announced that the Casbah had been named a world heritage location by Unesco, but that little had been done to date for its restoration. It had been, in the past, one of the finest examples of architecture from the Ottoman era, and had housed palaces decorated with pirate spoils from all over the Mediterranean. Even though it was now mostly a slum, housing ten families to each crumbling building, Janine longed to explore it. Normally she would have just hired a taxi and told the driver to take her there. But the impending arrival of Minister Haddad and her role in the woman's protection made her a bit more cautious than usual.

Cleaning out her briefcase she came across the embossed card from the gentleman from the airplane. He had mentioned the Cashah, and that he lived there. She wondered if it was worth dealing with his attentions to get a look at his neighborhood. She then called the Embassy to see if they were planning any escorted tours for diplomats and was told in no uncertain terms that it was 'off limits' for any American tourists. "We are unable to protect you there and we urge you not to go without a police escort and an official guide," she was told firmly and officially by a young aide to the Ambassador.

"And just how do I get a police escort?" Janine asked dryly.

"You apply to the Algerian Ministry of Tourism, but we understand that they are not encouraging visitors to go there at the moment."

"In other words you can't get there from here," Janine joked.

"Something like that," the young officer agreed, dryly.

Amir Zebur's invitation was looking better and better. What could happen to her in the middle of the day? She was armed and very used to Arab cities. She had lived in neighboring Tunisia and often frequented the Souks or Arab markets. This one was just older and not as well maintained. But she knew that she needed a guide. Otherwise she could wander around getting lost, and then she probably would get mugged, and miss the Minister's visit all together. She left a message on Rick's cell phone that she was going out to explore the city for a few hours and that she would leave her cell phone on in case he had any change in tomorrow's plans; then she called Amir Zebur's number from his card.

The phone was answered by a man's voice speaking in Arabic. Janine introduced herself in French and asked to speak to Monsieur Zebur. She was told that he was not at home, and the person answering did not know when he would return. He was away for the afternoon. "That is a shame," Janine replied, in her most charming voice. "He invited me to see his villa in the Casbah, and I am free this afternoon."

There was a moment's pause, then the person on the other end of the line passed the telephone to someone else. A woman's voice answered in impeccable French, "I am Madame Zebur, may I help you?"

Janine smiled. So she had caught Amir in one of his tricks. She decided to play the situation straight. "Your husband kindly invited me to visit your palace in the Casbah. He must have known that I am a student of Ottoman culture and artifacts. It is a shame that more of the palaces haven't been restored, such a disappointment for the UN cultural restorations," she let her voice taper off regretfully.

There was a long pause. Then the woman's voice murmured softly. "Then come and take tea with me this afternoon. It will be a pleasure to show you my home. I have so few visitors." She then repeated the address that Janine had on the card and told her that it was in the upper portion of the Casbah where a few of the ancient palaces had been partially restored. Tell the taxi driver to bring you to the upper gate, then ask him to accompany you to the top of the hill. No one will bother you if you are with an escort. I will be waiting for you at four o'clock," she said, then the telephone clicked off abruptly.

It didn't take Janine long to decide to accept Madame Zebur's invitation to visit her palace in the Casbah. She dressed carefully in a long caftan she had bought in Tunis, and tied a scarf around her hair. When the hour came, she walked to the front of the hotel and eyed the taxis standing there . It would be important to find one who would know the way to the Villa Zebur and who, for a promised tip, would help her find the Zebur's home and then wait for her till she finished her visit.

She was not long in finding candidates. All the drivers insisted that they knew the way, but she finally settled on the driver of a private car who was older and seemed responsible. He said his name was Ali that he knew the way to the villa, but told her in shocked tones that she should not try to enter the Casbah alone. He insisted that he must accompany her and wait for her while she made her visit. This arrangement suited Janine perfectly.

The drive through the winding streets was not long. Most of the architecture was dreary French colonial, featuring rusting, wrought iron balconies and graying facades. There seemed to have been no effort on the part of the government to make the city more attractive to tourists. But with billions of dollars a day pouring in from the sale of oil, Janine surmised that attracting tourists was not on their current agenda. The driver circled the Casbah until they came to an entrance not far from the top. The area had originally been built as a fortress and it hugged the side of a hill surrounded with a crumbling wall that had once, very long ago, made it impregnable. Now it just looked old and badly in need of repair.

Earthquakes and neglect had done what pirates and vandals couldn't accomplish. Now masses of tumbled and discolored stone announced where dwellings once had been. The driver parked outside a crumbling arched gate and ordered three boys, who were hanging around idly, to guard his car while he escorted Janine into the Casbah. Janine covered her hair with her scarf, and tucked her small purse, carrying her 9mm Beretta, securely under her arm. She planned to take no chances on the good will of the population or her hostess. She had entered a slum. The odors of rotting garbage and animal droppings assaulted her nose, which she covered with the loose end of her scarf. The driver looked around disapprovingly, and muttered his disgust in Arabic. He asked Janine politely if she wished to continue and seemed surprised when she answered 'Yes.'

The crumbling dwellings almost touched each other above them on the narrow cobblestone street, cutting off the sun. There were numerous jutting balconies, covered with thick latticework that had allowed the women of the Casbah to see but not to be seen. Janine had the feeling that unseen eyes were watching her every move, even now. She bent forward and followed her driver up a steep incline. At the top there was a slight view of the ocean and a breeze that cleared the air somewhat. Ali led her past a number of villas that had once been grand. Some seemed in the process of being rehabilitated. At a minimum, their facades had been whitewashed and the doors and decorations over the doorways had been repaired. Everywhere there was evidence of an era of lost elegance.

Ali indicated a house at the top of the cobblestone street and waited morosely while she lifted an ornate knocker, like a brass fist, and let it fall against the door. The ancient wood door gave a hollow sound as it hit, as though it hadn't been used in a long, long time. Janine waited, but there was no response. The driver looked at her questioningly. Janine shook her head and knocked again, twice. She could hear sounds from inside the building as though another door was being opened and then closed and bolted. The sounds were not very reassuring. The driver looked concerned but Janine nodded at him resolutely. She had come this far and she was not going back.

Finally the heavy wooden door opened slowly. Revealing a small wizened man about half of Janine's height, and dressed completely in white. He looked her up and down, taking in her caftan and the uniformed driver standing behind her. Then he nodded and gestured to Janine to come in. The driver indicated that he would wait outside for an hour as Janine had requested. Then he crouched down beside the door lighting a cigarette.

The servant, muttering his displeasure, closed the door firmly behind Janine and ushered her into a center courtyard with a burnished marble floor and a sparkling fountain in the middle. There were urns of bright bougainvillea in vivid oranges and pinks and fragrant jasmine surrounding the bubbling fountain. Janine felt as though she had stepped back in time, the contrast with the slum that she had just climbed through was extraordinary. Even the air smelled fresh here, the scent of garbage and animal dung was completely gone. Instead there was the heady scent of jasmine.

The servant ushered her into a small sitting room adjacent to the courtyard. It was simply, but elegantly, furnished with two golden brocade couches and a round copper table that held plates of assorted cakes and pastries. There was no sign of anyone else, no photographs or family memorabilia.

The old man nodded at her and slowly left the room. Janine began to be impatient. Had she willingly walked into a trap as Rick had suggested? She touched her purse and felt the comforting weight of her Beretta. After about ten more minutes she stood, and started back into the courtyard to look around. When a quiet voice behind her said gently, "Wouldn't you like to have your tea before you see the palace?"

She turned, somewhat taken aback, to see a white haired, elderly woman, elegantly dressed in a long turquoise silk *abaya,* leaning on a silver headed cane. Surely this could not be Amir's wife? Janine nodded, somewhat confused, and introduced herself. The woman's voice was the one that she had heard on the telephone, but Janine had expected a much younger woman.

The woman gestured graciously for Janine to sit down, and by some unseen signal on her part, the elderly servant carried in tea, presented in an antique silver tea service. Only when their fragile cups were filled with fragrant black tea did the woman speak again. "You were probably expecting someone younger as Madame Zebur. You see I am Amir's grandmother," she smiled shyly into her cup of tea. "But I do not get many visitors, and so I am afraid that I invited you under false pretences. I thought that I would enjoy showing someone from Unesco our restored villa."

Talk about false pretenses, Janine thought. She wasn't sure how the woman had gotten the impression that she was from the UN, but it seemed as though they were about equal at this point in misunderstandings. She sipped her excellent tea and ate a few of the delicious cakes, as the woman told her story.

She had married Amir's grandfather at the age of sixteen, just before the Algerian war broke out. They had known each other all their lives, as their fathers had been friends. Her father was a French planter and Amir's great grandfather, a rich merchant, had owned a number of palaces in the Casbah. "But then the war came," she said sadly. "The Casbah became a scene of destruction and torture, many innocent people were killed, among them my young husband. As a French girl married to an Algerian it was very difficult for me," she sighed. "Amir's family hid me until my baby was born. It was difficult," she sighed again and her eyes became opaque with tears, as if she was remembering terrible and lonely times. She sipped her tea slowly, looking out into the courtyard where the fountain was blowing in the afternoon breeze, spattering water onto the polished marble floor and the mosaics surrounding it.

" But as a French citizen, you could have returned to France with the other Pied Noir, couldn't you?" Janine asked, using the name that had been given to the thousands of French who were repatriated to France, a country which they barely new, after the Algerian war of independence ended in nineteen sixty two.

The old woman shook her patrician head slowly, and smiled sadly. "No, I had renounced my French citizenship in marrying Amir's grandfather. It was not a good time to be French in this country. It still is not. That is why I wear Arab clothing and that is why Amir has done so much to make this 'palace', as they call it, resemble the ones that he has seen in photographs." She looked around the elegant room proudly. "Everything was taken from us during the occupation and the following civil war. Vandals destroyed what was not stolen. I rarely leave this place now, but since you have finished your tea let me show you what my talented grandson had done to make an old woman happy."

She then rose to her feet and led Janine through room after room of priceless antique treasures. The rooms were adorned with elegant carpets and exquisite woodwork, decorated in gold and turquoise. Satin pillows in rainbow colors were tossed carelessly on gilded couches. Intricately carved tables held glass perfume bottles and braziers for incense. Everything was in exquisite taste. It was as if a loving hand had recreated a bygone era. Suddenly the old woman seemed to grow weary. She settled on one of the couches and patted the space beside her for Janine to sit. Janine glanced at the watch; she realized that much more than an hour had gone by, and she didn't want the driver to leave without her. Finding a taxi back from this location might not be easy.

She got up reluctantly and made her farewells, asking if she might come again and continue her visit. The old woman agreed, her eyes shining. "You see that these palaces are worth restoring. It is my dream to have the Casbah as beautiful and interesting as it once was before the war. I know that it will not happen before I die. But one can always hope. Your visit has much encouraged me." She said this holding Janine's hand in her fragile ones. "It has been such a long time since I have met anyone as sympathetic as you are. I would like to continue our acquaintance."

"May I come again?" Janine asked. There was still the matter of Amir's other life and how he had gained the money to furnish this palace so lavishly. But she would leave that question for later. She didn't want to involve this fragile woman in a controversy if there should be one. So she took her leave, promising to return at another time and deliberately leaving her relationship to Unesco an unanswered question.

The elderly servant ushered her to the front door, bowed from the waist and shut the door firmly behind her with a clang. Janine looked around for her driver, Ali, but he was nowhere to be seen. She was late, but not that late, and she was surprised that he hadn't waited for her as he had promised. He was going to miss a rather large tip.

She was pretty sure that she remembered the way to the gate they had entered from. It was downhill at any rate, and the first part of the walk was in bright sunlight. But the aspect changed radically as she entered one of the covered alleys that led sharply downhill. She was suddenly back in a slum and walking through dirty water and garbage. The odor was almost overpowering. Veiled women cast curious glances in her direction as she lifted the hem of her caftan up to keep it out of the dirty water. She could see the women looking at her foreign shoes, which were certainly not purchased in Algiers.

As she progressed down hill through the narrow street, she passed young men with seemingly nothing to do, lounging beside open doorways. She could see into some of the crumbling buildings that seemed to house dozens of people in their dimly lit rooms. Suddenly a donkey and driver blocked her way. She leaned against a wall to let the animal pass and was rewarded by an insolent stare from its owner. She rounded a corner and walked into an alleyway that turned out to be a dead end. The corner was filled with rubbish and with what looked like the putrefying body of a decaying animal. She backed out slowly, covering her mouth. Someone pushed against her from behind. She kicked backward, connecting with a leg and heard someone yelp in pain. She turned to confront one of the idle youths she had seen in a doorway. He leered at her making suggestive noises with his mouth.

Janine quoted a line of the Koran in Arabic about respecting your elders. The boy stood back for a moment, shocked, and allowed Janine to brush by him, her hand firmly on her purse. He attempted to grab it from her. But she was too quick for him. The Beretta was out in an instant and pointed at his face. "Leave me alone or even your mother won't recognize you", she hissed at him in Arabic. He made a grab for the gun, but Janine kicked him in the knee, disabling him long enough for her to get out of the alley. She then headed straight down through the filthy streets at a dead run, until she came to a gate. It was not the one that she had entered through, but at least it led to a main thoroughfare and sunlight.

She hiked slowly back up on the outside of the Casbah until she came to the gate she had started from. Ali was there, fiercely guarding his car from a gang of insolent teenagers. He smiled apologetically at Janine and was profuse in his explanations. She had been so long that he had been afraid to leave his vehicle any longer. He hoped that she understood and was not angry. In other words, would she still give him the promised extra tip? Janine was so relieved to crawl into the relative safety of the automobile, that she would have given him anything she owned at the moment. He looked at her disheveled appearance in the rear view mirror, and continued to apologize as they drove toward the hotel.

Janine made light of her adventure and assured him that her visit had been successful. "It had just taken longer than she had supposed it would. Yes, she would certainly hire him again if she needed transportation," she assured him. When they arrived at the hotel, she thanked him and tipped him generously and then tried to ignore the curious looks from the other hotel guests as she hurried through the lobby to the elevator, her room, and a much needed shower.

Her message light was blinking furiously when she entered her room. All the messages were from Rick, and he had gotten increasingly more agitated as the afternoon wore on. 'Where had she been, and why hadn't she checked in with him? They still had a number of things to clarify before tomorrow's visit. In the meantime, the international sponsors of the Bay of Algiers project were holding a reception this evening and he wanted her to attend with him. His company was looking at the loss of a half billion dollars if the project didn't go through. "That's right, billion," he said for emphasis, "if the deal was fouled up in any way." He wanted Janine to dress up and make nice this evening with the Germans and French who were designing the project, which was being bankrolled by the Algerians' oil money.

Janine hit 'delete' a number of times till all his messages were gone. Who did he think he was anyhow, trying to boss her around? Just because his company had paid for her plane ticket didn't give them an exclusive option on her time. Besides she had been working this afternoon. Amir was involved in something that was bringing him a great deal of money. He was working out of the Casbah, with the cover of his elegant French grandmother, whom he took care of, lavishly. But that wasn't all that was going on in his antique palace. Janine was sure of it. And she was determined to find out the rest of the story.

Chapter Twelve

When the phone rang, Janine ignored it and jumped into a hot shower. After washing her hair, and soaping off the odor of everything she had waded through this afternoon, she reluctantly dropped her favorite caftan into the wastebasket. There was no way that the smell of donkey dung would ever come out of the frayed and disgusting hem. She was sitting on the edge of the bed drinking a cold Perrier out of the room's small refrigerator, when the phone jangled again. She answered languidly, and kept her tone even while Rick restarted his tirade.

"Forget it," she said briskly. "I was working. Now what time is this shindig tonight and what shall I wear? I didn't bring much in my carry-on that would work for a cocktail party."

"I'll pick you up at seven," Rick replied coldly. "You can come naked as far as I am concerned. Though it might set the project back another few months."

Janine smiled wickedly into the phone. "Who knows, it might just push it forward, with all the Arabs dashing to get out of the room with a naked lady."

Fortunately the Hilton gift shop was prepared for just such emergencies. Janine picked out a nifty black sequined cocktail dress and charged it to her room. In her regular career, she didn't have much use for an outfit like this, so she decided to let Rick's company take it off as a business expense. Feeling pleased with herself, she donned black stockings, black strap sandals, fake diamond earrings and waited for Rick to call her from the lobby.

She didn't have to wait long before a loud knocking on her door announced his presence. She opened the door an inch at a time. He was brushed and polished and looking more angry than she had ever seen him. However, her recently purchased outfit caused him to pause and look her over carefully. "I said meet them, not seduce them," was his only comment as he ushered her out the door and down the hall to the elevator.

"Why the extra security?" Janine asked wryly, taking his arm.

"The hotel is crawling with a lot of Algerians that I would just as soon you not meet," Rick muttered, whisking her through the lobby. "You're going to be my secret weapon tomorrow and I don't want a lot of people checking you out beforehand."

"Thanks for the compliment," Janine muttered, climbing into Rick's rented limo, and catching the heel of her shoe as she did so. "Hell," she muttered, scooting over so that he could climb in beside her. "I'm sure that you wouldn't want me to arrive barefoot, putting this outfit together at the last minute was a drag."

"Don't fish for compliments," Rick scowled. "But you do look good enough to keep the 'big boys' attention."

"That was the general idea. Now do you mind telling me what's up?"

"We have a bit of a problem. The Algerians are thinking about backing out of the clean up project for Oued El Harrach. It will cost about half a billion dollars and much tighter controls for the factories along its banks, which are daily adding to the pollution and the high mercury levels. Some pretty powerful people are saying that the Bay of Algiers project can be built without cleaning up the river dumping into it. The Algerians have the money. The government earns about four billion a month selling their oil. The issue is really a long term environmental one. But they don't see it that way. They only see the inconvenience, plus the terrorist attacks on our site, aren't helping us any."

"So what so you want me to do?"

Rick glanced over at her appraisingly. "Do what you do so well. Schmoose some of the gentlemen, particularly the Algerian businessmen. See if you can find out who or what companies are behind this sudden resistance to the clean up. Give us an idea of where to start putting pressure."

Janine smiled wickedly. "That's all?"

"Should be enough for one evening, even for you." Rick quipped as their limo pulled up to a heavily guarded municipal building, with Algerian and French flags prominently displayed along the front balconies.

They were ushered through a line of smartly dressed police, evidence in itself of the importance of the occasion. There were a number of diplomatic cars disgorging their passengers, every woman more elegantly gowned than the one before. Janine was glad that Rick's company had splurged on her little black dress, even though they didn't know about it as yet. It was one more thing for Rick to be pissed off about when he got the bill. She didn't really care. This would not have been a good place to arrive in her tan cotton business suit. That would do for her outing with Minister Haddad.

They entered a lavish central hall, decorated with flowers and rounds of tables holding pitchers of fruit juice and cakes and pastries of every kind. In the center of the room was a huge mock up of the bay of Algiers project. White towered apartment buildings loomed over an artificial bay studded with miniature pleasure boats. It looked like something out of Dubai rather than Algeria. Janine surmised that was exactly the effect the Algerians wanted for their ambitious project.

White jacketed waiters passed glasses filled with colored drinks that Janine suspected were also non-alcoholic. This was after all an official event hosted by the Algerian government. The Koran must be obeyed and propriety respected publicly, no matter what happened in the privacy of their own homes and private men's clubs.

Rick guided her over to a group of men in the corner who looked somewhat hot and uncomfortable in their white dinner jackets. They were a group of the German engineers and designers of the project. Janine was quickly chatting with them in fluent German, which was her first language, since her mother had been born in Hamburg, and had made sure that her only child learned her native tongue. The Germans relaxed visibly under Janine's questioning. Rick nodded at her approvingly, but kept looking over her shoulder to identify the Algerian businessmen whom he wanted her to meet.

"Let me take you to get some refreshments," he said finally, taking her firmly by the arm.

She looked at up him, annoyed. She would make her way around the room in her own good time. She didn't need his help identifying people to talk with.

Just then she spotted Amir on the other side of the room. He was elegantly turned out and surrounded by a group of Algerian men dressed as he was, in perfectly cut dark suits and dinner jackets. They were standing somewhat apart from the rest of the guests, deep in conversation.

Janine nodded toward the group. "Why don't I go and say hello to my good friend Amir?" she said to Rick with a grin. "His group looks like a good place to start tonight. Why don't you come with me?" she added as an afterthought. "I'll introduce you to him."

Rick grimaced, but followed her across the room. She smiled invitingly at Amir and extended her hand. "I'm Janine Simms," she said brightly. At his astonished look, she continued graciously. "We met flying in from Paris yesterday. I'm sure that you remember, you offered me a ride to my hotel." The Algerian looked at her grimly, and then decided to play along with Janine's game, whatever it was. He took her hand, and shook it, then stood quietly looking over at Rick for an introduction. He was on much safer ground dealing with a man. Janine introduced Rick as her 'colleague,' which forced Amir to also introduce his companions, who were obviously not pleased to have their private conversation interrupted by two unknown foreigners.

Several of the men moved away, but three of them stayed, watching Janine out of hooded eyes. They weren't sure if she was flirting with Amir in front of her male companion or if she was just an American woman without manners or a knowledge of women's place in society. Janine continued to talk to Amir as if they were old friends. Telling him about her visit to his grandmother. He looked taken aback at the information that she was the woman who had visited his home earlier in the day. "But my grandmother said that her visitor was from Unesco," he answered grimly.

"A simple misunderstanding," Janine continued warmly." I only told her that I was interested in antiquities. She was kind enough to show me some of the treasures in your collection."

Amir's look said that he would like to strangle her. " How kind of you to say so," he answered grimly. "Would you mind telling us what you are really doing here?"

"Visiting with friends and enjoying the country," Janine answered brightly, sipping her drink. " I am somewhat interested in the water purification project for Oued El Harrach, which I hear will be a milestone for the city."

One of the men began to protest, visibly angered. But a look from Amir silenced him.

"There are a number of different opinions on that project," he said charmingly. "Many of the businesses represented in this room feel that it would be a huge risk of our resources and bound to failure. Especially since the families that live along its banks are in the habit of using it as a sewer."

"And a place to do their washing and get drinking water too, I understand," Rick said in an even tone. "Certainly the health benefits of clean water to that population would be enormous."

"We are not here to look after the health of squatters along the river's banks at the expense of our factories," a heavy-set man who had been listening intently to the conversation, hissed in Arabic.

"But certainly the health of Algeria's children is important?" Janine responded in English.

The man looked astonished and then angry. "Who are you foreigners to tell us what we can't do," he replied in heavily accented French. " I myself did not invite you to visit my country and display yourself," he said looking directly at Janine's short skirt and bare arms. "You corrupt our society." With that he turned his back and walked away. Leaving Janine and Rick with Amir and one other man who up until now had said nothing. He had been listening to the conversation and nodding occasionally.

Now he spoke "There is nothing that you can do to change our ways. They say that our factories pollute, but they want the products that we produce and the foreign exchange that we bring in. *Inshalla,* it is all in the hands of Allah, and it would be well for you foreigners not to interfere." He used a pejorative term in Arabic for 'foreigner' one that was sure to offend. Then he looked defiantly at the Americans, turned his back and strode away.

"Well, that went well," Janine said brightly.

"You have offended my friends," Amir said bluntly. "For what purpose?"

"To hear what I just heard," Janine answered honestly. "You and your friends do not want the purification project to continue. Now the question is would you commit a criminal offense to stop it?"

"We are not criminals," Amir said tightly." We have other ways to influence what is done and not done in our country," he nodded at Rick and then turned his back and followed his friends to the other side of the room.

" Is that your version of diplomacy?" Rick asked grimly.

"No, but you found out what you wanted to know, didn't you?"

He shook his head, leading her back toward the center of the room. "Try to be a little more subtle with any more of your interrogations this evening, if possible," he said, pulling her over to meet a group of French engineers.

The rest of the evening went well. Janine had decided to be charming. So she flirted with the engineers in fluent French and was rewarded by several invitations for lunch the following day. Invitations, which she regretfully refused because of the Minister's pending arrival.

She caught sight of Amir several times, watching her from the other side of the room. His eyes were furious and seemed to bore through her flimsy dress. Her legs were beginning to ache from standing so long on high heels, which she rarely wore these days, because of her height. She found that it made men uncomfortable for her to tower over them. Perhaps that was what had made Amir so angry. He had certainly reacted strongly to her questions. She doubted if he was also a factory owner. She suspected that his income was from other sources not quite so legitimate.

When they arrived back at the hotel, much later that evening, she refused Rick's offer of a nightcap in the hotel's well appointed bar. Her legs ached from the party and her day's exertion in the Casbah. So she told Rick goodnight and promised to see him at breakfast for a briefing on the security preparations for the Minister's visit, which the Algerians were still finalizing. She took the elevator to her room, looking forward to a warm bath and a soft drink from the mini bar. Her key stuck in the door because it was already open by a hair's breath. She shoved open the door, her body on alert and her Beretta drawn out of her evening bag.

The room was empty. It had been searched, but not expertly. Her laptop was smashed and her suitcase left open.

Her personal belongings were strewn around the room as though someone wanted her to show her that her privacy had been violated. Her lipstick had been used to write inflammatory words in Arabic on her bathroom mirror. It was clear that someone did not welcome her visit to Algiers.

Chapter Thirteen

Rick called her room bright and early. Janine had stayed up late going through her belongings and had ascertained that very few items were missing. Her passport and visa were in the hotel safe, and the other items that had been taken were more to annoy her than anything else. Her computer was a wreck. Someone had tried to access her encrypted files and in doing so had addled its brains completely. She would have to have it totally cleaned and then start over when she got back to Paris. She wasn't communicating with anyone important via e-mail at the moment. Non-secure e-mails could be sent using the hotel computer reserved for the guest's use.

But the message on her mirror made her angry. She was here to help avoid an international incident involving Minister Haddad. That was her only purpose. That and identifying a few terrorist leaders if possible. But that was the other half of her job. Not one that she was apt to make much progress on in the short time she was in Algiers.

Rick came up to her room with a sheaf of papers and more information on his Blackberry. He looked somewhat taken aback at the room's disarray. "I had some visitors last night while we were out," Janine said grimly. "It seems I'm not one of their favorite people at the moment."

"Good thing you're not staying long."

Janine shrugged. "Let's see the plans for today," she said, offering him a cup of coffee from her room service tray. "I promise to keep my head down and do whatever I can to protect the Minister, she seems like my kind of person."

"Sorry that's not true for everyone. She has ruffled quite a lot of feathers at home."

"I told you that I liked her." Janine answered, biting into a warm brioche, while she looked over the plans Rick spread out beside her breakfast tray.

Rick's company was clearly taking no chances with their part of the tour. The site for the Bay of Algiers project was gigantic, covering acres of undeveloped property, and old warehouses. Any one of them an ideal place for a group planning an attack or to take hostages. Rick's plan was simple. They would pick up the convoy at a certain point early in the official visit. That way Minister Haddad could tour the prospective site for the water purification plant early in the afternoon. This was one of her reasons for the visit as it also included tearing down a number of slums along the river's bank and replacing them with affordable housing. This was exactly the sort of project that she was so vocally involved with in Paris.

Janine's job was to ride with her during this part of the visit, to serve as a representative of Rick's company and more importantly, to protect her from a possible attack or attempt to kidnap her. " I don't mind telling you that this whole visit is a nightmare." Rick said, pouring himself another cup of scalding black coffee.

"I see that," Janine said studying the Minister's route on a map spread out on her hastily made bed. " If she asks to make a detour we are in trouble. I assume that there isn't any way that you can cover all contingencies?"

"Nope, it's your job to see that she stays on track at all times, at least on our site. The Algerians are in charge of the rest of her program and I just hope that they have her covered as well as we do," he said, rubbing the back of his neck. "Your driver is a crack shot and we will be tracking your progress continually, as well as preceding and following your car with armed guards and company personnel. But she is going to want to get out to see the site from our construction tower. That's the point that is making the rest of my hair turn gray. I want you to stick to her like molasses. Are you armed?"

Janine took the Beretta out of her evening bag. "Fortunately, they didn't get this. I had it with me last evening."

"I'm surprised that you didn't plug one of those guys that was giving you grief at the party last night."

Janine grinned and studied the map more carefully. "You have tried to limit accessibility to the Minister. But I see too many places where things could go wrong," she said, running her hands through her newly washed hair.

"Well, this is just the peliminary route. They were still haggling over it when I left the Algerians in charge of her visit this morning. After all, she is just a Minister, not the President, and a woman. I'm not sure how serious they are about protecting her against all contingencies. That's where we come in."

"I'm glad you said 'we'" Janine answered, finishing the dregs of her coffee. "I don't feel up to taking on al Qaida all by my self today."

"Not a problem," Rick said confidently. "Better get suited up and I will take you to the official briefing."

****

The official plan changed a dozen times during the morning. Rick was adamant that his company's portion would not change and that it would stay strictly on schedule. This is why his company had insisted that the Minister visit their construction site early. It was easy to get behind in these affairs and they didn't want to have to show her around late in the day, when the sun was going down and visibility would be more difficult.

Janine was dressed in her appropriate beige suit and low heels. She carried a brown leather purse over her shoulder that had plenty of room for her weapon, which she planned to stow in the back of her belt under her jacket, when her time to accompany the Minister arrived. The plane from Paris was late, which threw the whole planning process into chaos. But Rick held his ground, insisting that the visit to his company's site would come right after the official greeting had taken place at the airport.

They waited on the outside of the tarmac for over an hour while the plane landed and the Algerian officials greeted the Minister. She was dressed in a dark suit and wore a *hajab*, or headscarf in deference to the Algerians who had come to meet her. Janine suspected that she rarely, if ever, wore one in France. She was more slender than Janine remembered, having only seen her once, and that from a distance. She carried herself as though she was taller and her eyes were dark and penetrating. She took in the scene and everyone who had come to meet her, while she made polite remarks in Arabic to the Algerians who were welcoming her.

After the official greetings were over, Rick went forward with his team and introduced himself and Janine, who would accompany the Minister in the touring car. Haddad sized Janine up with one glance and seemed pleased with what she saw. She eased herself gracefully into the right seat of company's waiting car. Janine slid into the left side, and introductions followed. Then Janine handed her an outline of the day's program with a detailed sketch of the proposed purification plant and low income housing along the river's banks.

Jalila, for that is what she had asked Janine to call her, asked a number of questions in a low musical voice. Janine was happy that she was such a quick study and that she was able to answer most of them intelligently. Rick had placed an additional burly guard to ride in front beside the driver. There was also an alarm button on the left side of the floor, which Janine was to press if she sensed any trouble, or needed help during the tour. The preparations seemed almost to be overkill in Janine's estimation. But one could never be too careful, not now, not in the Arab world.

The motorcade, for that is what it had now become, drove slowly through the construction site. Workmen stopped and stared as the cars went by, but Janine didn't sense any hostility, mostly curiosity, that such a long train of official cars should drive through the rubble of a construction site. Several times the cars slowed so that the Minister could look out the window at a special section of the building construction. But Janine made sure that the car windows remained up and the doors locked, despite the increasing heat in the vehicle.

The Minister seemed uncomfortable with the extreme security. After all, this was the land of her parent's birth and she was anxious to make contact with some of its citizens. Janine almost had to restrain her from opening the door at one of the stops to talk with the workmen, by promising her that she would soon have a bird's eye view of the whole site from one of the viewing towers.

The tower soon came into view. The official cars parked in a circle around it, so that there was no chance of anyone interrupting the Minister's viewing. She exited gracefully from the car with Janine close behind her, and the guard following Janine. There was a small elevator at the foot of the tower, with only room for two people. Jalila entered with Janine right behind her. The burly guard waited at the bottom till both were aloft, where they exited onto a railed balcony, with a panoramic view of the construction site with the Bay of Algiers in the distance. Jalila took off the *hajab* and shook her short hair loose in the wind. She smiled at Janine, and then leaned over the balcony, enjoying the view.

Just then a shot rang out, and then another. Instinctively Janine pushed the Minister to the floor and covered her slender body with her own, while grabbing for her Beretta. Shouts came from below and another shot. Then the elevator arrived carrying the heavy-set guard. He threw himself down beside the two women and began to return fire. It was impossible to know where the shots were coming from. The popping sounds were coming from below, from both sides of the tower. Janine had her weapon out and was covering the Minister whom she kept pushed flat on the deck, despite the woman's muffled protests.

Janine could hear shouts and confusion from below. The Algerians were yelling at one another, and waving their arms in distress. She could see Rick below covering the entrance to the elevator with his weapon out. Suddenly her cell phone shrilled. She pulled it gingerly from her pocket, with one arm still protectively around Jalila, and held it to her ear.

It was Rick, sounding grim. "We still haven't identified the source of the shots. Stay where you are, and keep your heads down. I don't want to risk the elevator again until we know that everything is clear. How is the Minister?"

"Not happy" Janine said tersely. She had helped the frightened woman to crawl behind a construction pillar at the back of the viewing deck, so that she could stand upright. But she was clearly upset at being shot at. She had retied the *hajab* around her hair.

"Not exactly the welcome that I was expecting from my countrymen," she murmured ruefully in French. " I had expected some conflict, but nothing like this."

"There are elements in this country who don't want this project to go forward," Janine said tersely. "That is why the security here has been so tight."

"But that is no reason to use me for target practice. I am French/Algerian."

"I'm afraid that it is the French part they don't like. Your presence here makes the project more important. It seems to give it the approval, or at least the interest, of France. That is something that the competing interests can't abide."

The Minister looked thoughtful. " Is that why they sent a woman to protect me?"

"Something like that."

Jalila smiled, showing perfect white teeth, and making her look suddenly younger. "Well, I must thank you for doing such an excellent job. Even if I must change my pantyhose when I get down," she said, showing Janine a large tear at the knee.

Janine nodded ruefully, her pantsuit was also torn at the knees. Then her phone rang again. It was Rick, giving a cautious all clear. "We caught one guy, but there may be others. You can use the elevator but crouch down well below the windows as you do," he said grimly. "Have the big guy stay on the deck and cover you from above. We don't want to take any chances. I have a dozen guys here prepared to shoot on sight."

"Just make sure that they point their guns in the right direction." Janine answered softly. "I think that we've both had enough excitement for one day. Besides the Minister needs to change her torn panty hose, before her next meeting."

Chapter Fourteen

Back at the hotel that evening, Janine stripped off her filthy suit. She had already ruined most of the clothes that she had brought with her in her carry-on bag. The hotel shop didn't carry much of anything but bathing suits and evening clothes, at an extraordinary price. She had a feeling that she might have exceeded Rick's budget for her hotel stay. But her clothes had all been ruined in the line of duty and there were still two days to go of this long weekend.

The rest of the Minister's afternoon had gone quietly. The Algerians had indicated that it was because she was with them and better protected, both Janine and Rick had taken offence at their pointed remarks. Six Algerian soldiers had just been killed by rebels about sixty miles from Algiers, and their uniforms and weapons taken. That had put the Algerian security forces on high alert. Kidnapping the Minister would be a great prize and they were taking no chances that this might happen. Janine was relieved to be officially off duty. She had had enough excitement for one day and she had a feeling that the Minister had too. But Jalila was obliged to go through with the rest of the official visit. Rick and Janine probably wouldn't see her again until the final reception, which was to take, place at the end of her visit tomorrow.

According to Rick, his company was disturbed at what had happened at their construction site, despite all of their extra precautions, but they weren't surprised. Theories abounded about who the attackers might have been. Now the man who had been apprehended was in the custody of the Algerian authorities, and there was still no news about what group he was connected to.

"Probably al Qaida in North Africa, as they call themselves now," Rick said grimly, in the hotel bar, over his afternoon drink. "At least they didn't harm her."

Janine looked at him speculatively, "If you don't call getting shot at, blooding your knees and ruining a pair of panty hose 'harm.'"

"Forget the panty hose,"Rick grinned. "Overall you did a good job of protecting her."

"But we are no closer to whoever is heading up the operation."

"And we may not ever be. Unless the Algerians can use some of their very persuasive methods to find out who hired the assassin they have in custody."

"So you know that there were at least two?"

Rick shook his head ruefully, "Unless the same guy was running back and forth to both sides of the tower."

"About that tower," Janine said, sipping her drink. "Whose great idea was it anyhow to take her up there. It made us both sitting ducks."

"Blame the guys in New York," Rick said, crossing his long, jean clad, legs, " They wanted her to have a safe view of the whole project, and the whole place was crawling with security guards."

"Could it have been two of them that shot at us?"

"Bingo," Rick said, taking her hand gently. "Where did you get your powers of deduction?"

" It's what we specialize in at the company," Janine said removing her hand from his, and standing up slowly, painfully aware of her bruised knees.

"How about finishing up this conversation upstairs?" Rick asked, smiling up at her and taking hold of the hand that held her room key.

"Why don't you hold that thought till we get out of this situation," Janine said softly.

"You may have second thoughts when we get back to Paris."

"Hey, we may not live that long," Rick teased. "My grandma always said, 'tomorrow isn't promised you, my dear.'"

"Well, I'll think about it, tomorrow," Janine said slowly. "Now I'm going up to order dinner in my room."

"Well, if a man calls later, don't hang up. It will be me."

Chapter Fifteen

The phone did ring later in the middle of the night. At least that's what Janine thought she heard. "What?" she answered groggily, getting ready to blast whoever it was for waking her.

It was Rick's voice, but it wasn't the invitation that she was expecting. "Roll out of bed sweetheart," he said in a gruff voice. "You are back on duty."

"In the middle of the night?"

"Nope, it's five am and the Minister wants to take a tour into the mountains to get a closer look at the countryside she's heard so much about and see the Roman ruins at Timgad. Guess who she wants beside her in the car as an escort?"

Janine uttered a word she wouldn't say in polite company. Then, "Why me?" she moaned. "I'm not even part of her official escort party."

"Seems she thinks that you are, and the Algerians aren't about to confuse her with the facts. They don't have many charming armed women, like you, who can escort her."

"Thanks for the charming," Janine groaned. "What time do we leave and do I get extra pay for this? I'm not sure that it's in my contract."

"I'm sure that it isn't, but think of the brownie points you will get from the agency for spending this much time alone in the back seat of the car with the Minister. You can interrogate her for hours."

"How many hours?"

"About five to get there and back, and another two or three to walk around and have lunch. You should make quite a day of it. By the way you leave in an hour."

Janine ordered coffee and a croissant and rolled out of bed, aching in every muscle. Her right knee didn't bend too well and her shoulder had a catch in it. "I'm getting too old for this sort of work," she groaned as she stood briefly under the scalding shower, which she then switched to icy cold to finish job of waking up.

She dressed in her last clean shirt and the rumpled pant's suit from yesterday. Thinking better of it, when she saw the hole in the knee of the right trouser leg, she changed to jeans and the beige jacket that covered her weapon. Drinking her coffee hurriedly, she left the cup at the registration desk as a long, official looking limo pulled up in front of the hotel.

The Minister was in the back seat, bright as a button and ready to go at this ungodly hour. She was wearing a tailored pant's suit with a bright *hijab* tied around her neck. She smiled gratefully at Janine, as her protector, climbed into the back seat beside her. Jalila looked as delighted as a child on a birthday outing. "I hope that you will forgive me for asking for you at the last minute. But the Algerian authorities were reluctant to let me leave Algiers without protection in the car with me. A man would not have been appropriate in their eyes," she confided. "After yesterday's demonstration, I convinced them that you could more than take care of me."

"Well, I hope that we I have some backup?" Janine said glancing behind them, where a jeep, with several armed soldiers lounging in the front seat was idling.

"Some of Algeria's finest," Rick said, sticking his head through the car window. "But with the gift of a couple of packs of cigarettes, I've convinced them to let me ride along with them."

Janine smiled at him gratefully. He was a good man to have around in an emergency. She was surprised that the Algerians had agreed to let their guest go into the mountains as far as Timgad. It was in an isolated region, which was one of the reasons that it had not been totally ruined by vandals and later by tourists. It was now a world heritage site and somewhat protected because of that. Also by the fact that few tourists were allowed in this region, because the government didn't want the responsibility of protecting them. Janine wondered again why the authorities were allowing the Minister to travel there today. Perhaps they were just glad to get rid of her for the day. It cut down on the cost of official receptions in her honor and seemed to make her happy to see the country of her grandparent's birth.

The caravan took a circuitous route out of the city and then on to a road that led into rolling green hills beyond it. Janine began to relax a bit. She knew that there could be an ambush anywhere along their route today. But as they made their way into the hills they saw few people along the road. The few dwellings they passed were mostly set back from the road and were clean but shabby looking. She saw a few scrawny goats grazing idly along the way with an occasional ragged boy looking after them. The Minister gazed out of the window, lost in her own thoughts, so Janine didn't need to make conversation.

Once or twice, Janine eased her position to adjust her aching knee and Jalila looked over at her curiously. Her face looked less pinched today: she seemed younger. As though this trip back into her family's past was an unexpected gift. Janine only hoped that the day wouldn't turn out to be a disappointment, or a disaster.

They stopped at Batna, a town about twenty-five miles from the ruins, to take a bathroom break. It was an ugly town of square whitewashed buildings, constructed by the French as an army garrison in 1884 according to the guide book. It looked as though not much had changed in it since then. The buildings were utilitarian. The few hotels looked as though they had seen somewhat better days. Fortunately, someone had thought to pack a picnic lunch and Janine and the Minister had sandwiches and lemonade in the car, parked in the shade, while the driver ate a kebab from a roadside vendor. They went into the hotel bar to wash their hands afterward and were met by curious looks. The Minister had tied her head scarf around her hair, but Janine went in bare headed and was rewarded by the insolent stares of the few men in the bar at this time of the morning.

The proprietor, however, was more solicitous, giving them towels to wipe their hands and offering them a warm carbonated drink. Jalila accepted the towels, but refused the drinks politely in Arabic. The man watched the women curiously as they climbed back into the car.

Rick was pointedly staying with the soldiers. Attempting to find out where they were from and what their orders were for the day. The young men were taciturn and somewhat sullen. They obviously didn't think that guarding two women on a joy ride was much of a military maneuver. Rick was doing his best to jolly them along, offering them cigarettes and speaking to them in his very basic Arabic. Janine was grateful for his presence. Though she would never have admitted it to him.

After the short rest stop, the vehicles started up the hill toward Timgad. The area rapidly became more and more desolate. Janine could see why tourists seldom came here, despite the amazing Roman ruins that awaited them. The Arabs weren't very interested in their Roman past except to decorate their mosques with marble pinched from the temples. The Aures Mountains weren't impressive to American eyes, used to the Rockies. But the air was cooler and had a clean wind swept smell.

The first glimpse of the ruins was breathtaking. Yellowing marble temples seemed to cascade down the valley below them, surrounded by utter silence. Not even a bird stirred in the underbrush. It was as if the town had been waiting for them through the centuries. An elderly guard of sorts came toward them bowing and salaaming as they got out of the limo to stretch their legs. Jalila looked delighted and began to speak with him in rapid Arabic, which Janine could barely follow. But she did get the impression that the Minister's grandparents had come from somewhere in this region and that she was asking the old man something about them. He shook his head sadly several times and pointed to the hills beyond. "*Les Francais*," the French, he said morosely, and made a cutting gesture with his hand across his throat.

Jalila thanked him and then translated for Janine. "He says that the French took the people's animals, their lively hood, and that forced them to leave," she said bitterly. "It was the same all over. My parents were lucky to get to France with their lives. They had nothing else. But they always dreamed of returning to this valley." she sighed. "It was their only real home. In France, they always felt like displaced persons."

She let the old man guide them through the ruins, since he had taken them on as his 'clients.' He spoke primarily in a dialect of Arabic which Janine could barely understand. But she was content to look around her at the magnificent site. Rick and the two bored looking soldiers followed close behind. Janine insisted that they stay on the main paths where she had a clear view of what was coming their way at all times. She had no reason to distrust the old man. But it was her experience that anyone could be bought for a price. Especially in a region as poor as this one.

By noon the two women were hot and exhausted. The sun had come up with a vengeance and even the head scarves which they now wore as protection against it only made them hotter. Janine suggested politely that they return to the Limo for lunch and something cool to drink. Jalila agreed reluctantly. It was as though she had bonded with the old man and with the landscape and was loath to leave it. Even though she did not connect with the Roman past, Janine could see that this visit meant something very special to the Minister. She seemed both saddened and exhilarated by it. She walked slowly back up the hill murmuring her thanks to the old man. Janine tipped him and thanked him in French politely. He glanced at her briefly. And just for a moment Janine saw something in his expression that put her on guard.

She signaled to Rick that they should be ready to go after a quick lunch. He nodded agreement. There was something in the absolute stillness of the place that was unnerving. Even the elderly guide had disappeared. The soldiers felt it too. They became more alert and held their weapons at the ready, looking around cautiously. One even fired off a shot at a stray rattle in the bushes. Rick silenced him with a look. There was no reason to telegraph their presence in this isolated spot. Even though, after their rest stop in Batna, probably a number of people already knew that they were visiting the site.

There was an answering gunshot from off in the distance. It could mean nothing. But it could also be some kind of signal. This was an isolated spot with only one navigable road. Not a good place to be caught, especially while guarding the Minister. Janine wondered again why they had been given such light protection. In her experience official visits were usually crawling with armed bodyguards. She touched her Beretta, making sure that the safety was off. Then she gave an order to the driver to proceed down the hill toward Batna as rapidly as was safe on this ancient rutted road.

There were more shots. This time they were closer. Looking behind her, Janine could see the two soldiers with their machine guns pointed in the direction of the shots. Though with the echoes of the valley, it was hard to tell exactly from which direction they were coming. The driver of the Jeep was following the limo as close as possible while keeping his head down and gunning the motor. When they came to a wide place in the road the jeep zoomed around and in front of the limo. Rick gave Janine a warning look and a 'heads down' signal as they passed.

Janine now had a protesting Jalila huddled on the limo floor. She was crouched beside her, just high enough so that she could see out the window and keep her gun pointed at the road. They were eating the jeep's dust now and it made it harder to see. The sound of shooting came nearer and nearer. It was almost upon them, but the road was covered with clouds of dust so that it was impossible to see their attackers.

Jalila muttered a protest, but Janine kept her hand on the Minister's shoulder. Keeping her in the relative safety of the limo's floor. She knew that if the cars were attacked from all sides no one was really safe. She swore at herself for taking this assignment. They had really set themselves up as moving targets for al Qaida. Just then, through the noise of gunshots, she began to hear the faint sound of music. It became louder and louder and almost drowned out the shots. She saw Rick in the Jeep ahead of them, shake his head and drop his weapon to his side as he turned back to look at her with a wide grin.

In a moment, she saw the cause of his amusement. An Algerian wedding party was crossing the road in front of them. The bride was carried in a covered throne-like chair on the shoulders of her male relatives. The rest of the party surrounded the chair, talking and laughing and shooting off their ancient weapons. Women, their hands red with henna dye, walked behind making the high-pitched yodel that indicated celebration in the Arab world. Behind them sauntered musicians beating on drums and jangling instruments.

The jeep came to a skidding stop, followed closely by the limo. Soon both vehicles were surrounded by laughing and shouting Algerians, with their hands out asking for money for the bride. Rick threw down some coins shouting congratulations in Arabic. Jalila pulled herself up from the floor of the limo, grimacing at Janine and immediately joined Rick in tossing coins out the window toward the bride's caravan shouting congratulations, *mabruk!*

After that, the ride back to Algiers was uneventful. Janine was tired and so was the Minister, who had retreated into a thoughtful silence, occasionally glancing out the window at the passing scenery. They didn't stop until they got back to the hotel and deposited the Minister with her official Algerian welcoming committee. Janine knew that there would be a farewell dinner this evening. But thankfully, she had not been invited. She was grateful, because she wanted to make one last visit to the Casbah in the morning to follow up on her curiosity about Amir Zebur.

She needed some time to think through how she was going to make that happen. Her flight for Paris left in the late afternoon, and she knew that Rick expected her to be on it with him. But something about Amir's palace in the Casbah really troubled her. It was all too perfect amid the surrounding desolation. There had to be a reason for the display of so much wealth and ostentation in such a poverty stricken area. And she meant to find out what it was before she left Algiers .

Chapter Sixteen

After politely refusing Rick's invitation to dinner, Janine ate alone in her room. She planned to get up early and say goodbye to Jalila, if she was lucky enough to catch her in the hotel lobby before the early flight left for Paris the next morning. She dressed hurriedly in her new gray and white caftan from the hotel shop, and a headscarf and was amused to see Jalila's surprised look as she shook her hand in parting.

"Please call me when you get back to Paris," the Minister said earnestly. "Let me know if there is ever anything I can do to help you."

"I will let you know if I am looking for work as a security guard," Janine replied, smiling and shaking her hand. "Have a safe trip home."

The minute that the official limos left for the airport, Janine began to plan her trip to the Casbah. It was much too early to telephone an elderly woman. Besides she was sure that Amir had probably warned his grandmother not to invite her back again, giving some obscure reason. But she had felt a real warmth for the lonely old woman. And she was really looking forward to seeing her again, despite her suspicions about her grandson. She picked out a lovely turquoise silk and gold-flecked scarf from the hotel shop and had it gift wrapped. It would serve as parting gift in gratitude for the elderly woman's hospitality. A gift would not seem out of place and would give her an excellent reason to visit the palace again this morning.

Pleased with herself, she had a strong cup of coffee in the hotel café while she waited for it to be late enough to visit. She kept her head covered and her face down. She didn't want to run the risk of meeting anyone that she knew and having to explain why she was dressed like an Arab woman.

To make the time go faster, she went back up to her room and made sure that her bags were packed and that she had left out something to wear on the plane. Thinking it through, she put on jeans and a tee shirt under the caftan. It for some reason she was late getting back she could add her beige jacket and wear her jeans onto the plane. Finally it was just barely late enough for a social visit. She left a message for Rick that she has gone to do some last minute shopping and that she would be back well in time to catch their flight.

As usual, there was a crowd of taxies waiting for tourists in front of the hotel, but she didn't see her former limo driver. She asked one of the other drivers about him and was told that he didn't come on until after lunch. He had another job in the morning. The man spoke French and said that he knew the Casbah like the back of his hand. His uncle still lived there. He would make sure that Madame got there and back safely. Janine decided to take a chance on him, since this time she knew pretty much where she was going.

The sun was bright on the Mediterranean this morning. Whitewashed buildings clustered along the coast looked picturesque in the fierce morning light. Janine could see that if you didn't get close enough to smell the poverty, this could eventually turn into a resort town attracting the jet setters of the world. But that was a long time off. Rick's clean up project would help as well as would the new marina and the luxury villas planned along the harbor. But there were lots of hurdles to jump over before that was accomplished. The clearing out of al Qaida in North Africa should be on the government's short list.

Her train of thought was interrupted by the driver's hair raising drive around the outskirts of the Casbah. Fortunately there weren't too many other cars in evidence. But there were plenty of motor bikes and bicycles. The driver almost collided with a wagon, loaded with melons, pulled by a discouraged looking donkey. The driver blew his horn violently, causing the donkey to bolt and the wagon to almost overturn. Fortunately it righted itself at the last minute. Janine didn't look forward to having to purchase a load of melons with what was left of her Algerian money.

There were no more incidents before they arrived at the entrance to the upper Casbah. Janine paid the driver and promised him a very large tip if he would wait for her for an hour. He promised, but then insisted on accompanying her up a steep path that led to the upper Casbah. He did seem to know where he was going and they arrived at the palace in record time, traveling a more direct route than the one that she had traveled before. Janine still felt as though she should be dropping bread crumbs to find her way back, as the heroines did in the German fairy tales her mother read to her as a child.

The sun was high now and it gleamed on the polished brass knocker on the front door of the Zebur's palace. The door was now painted a bright blue. Possibly to ward off the evil eye, or perhaps just to keep unwelcome visitors like herself, at bay. Janine knocked firmly, clutching her gift in one hand and feeling the welcome weight of her Beretta against her hip. There was no answer to her first knock, so she knocked again, louder this time, and was rewarded by the shuffling sound of someone coming slowly to answer the door. It was the same ancient retainer who had opened the door on her first visit. He looked at her suspiciously, barring her way with his frail body.

"Is Madame Zebur at home? I have a farewell gift for her," Janine announced in her most flowery Arabic. "I am returning home today."

The old man hesitated, shaking his head as though he didn't understand. But Janine was insistent. "I am leaving for Paris this afternoon and I just want to say goodbye to your employer. See I have a gift for her," she said, holding out the beautifully wrapped package.

Perhaps it was the hotel's elaborate gift wrapping that decided him. He opened the door just wide enough for Janine to enter and then reached out to take the package. But Janine wasn't going to make it that easy for him. "I must give it to Madame myself," she said, edging her body forward into the outside courtyard. " I can wait here if she is not yet awake."

"Sleep is for the young," came a musical voice from one of the upper balcony. Janine looked up and saw the elderly woman fully dressed and smiling, leaning over an ornate balcony. "Come up and have a cup of coffee with me. I will enjoy your company at breakfast."

Janine glanced at her watch. It was now eleven o'clock. She was glad that she hadn't come any earlier since 'Madame' was still at breakfast. But this gave her an excellent chance to take a look at the upper rooms of the palace, if she could somehow manage it. She climbed a steep set of marble stairs to the upper balcony. The rooms were arranged in a 'u' shape around the lower floor. The parquet floors were badly cracked and still in need of repair. But the elderly servant ushered her into a sumptuous bedroom, adorned with embroidered silk hangings. The elderly woman smiled up at her from her breakfast table, an elaborate copper tray balanced on three spindly legs. It held a silver coffee service, a mug of hot milk and a pile of buttery croissants.

Seeing Janine's look of surprise the elderly woman smiled, showing perfect teeth. "You see I still breakfast 'a la Francais,' childhood habits are hard to break. I have even taught my cook how to bake croissants and brioche. Please join me in a café au lait."

Janine accepted eagerly. Her quick snack in the hotel restaurant early this morning had left her longing for a good cup of coffee. She was not disappointed. Amir must certainly spoil his grandmother in many ways. She said so, just to make conversation, and was rewarded with another smile.

"My grandson is very generous," the elderly woman agreed. " But what brings you back here so early in the morning?" she said charmingly. "Did you want to see more of the restorations of the palace?"

"I certainly would," Janine replied honestly. Surprised at how easy this was becoming. "But since I am leaving this afternoon for Paris, I wanted to give you a small gift to thank you for your kind hospitality to a tourist and a stranger." She then held out the package in its elaborate hotel wrapping.

The old woman shook her head shyly. " But I have nothing to offer you in return," she said, holding the package unopened in her fragile hands.

"Your friendship is my gift" Janine replied hastily, realizing that she had unwittingly committed a breach of protocol. In the Arab world a gift must be returned with a gift of equal value to the giver, or the recipient remained in the other's debt. This was not at all what she had intended.

But the old woman smiled gently as though she had just thought of the solution. Then she unwrapped the gift carefully, folding the paper and ribbon and putting it on a side table to be saved. She exclaimed with delight at the glistening *hijab* and immediately tied it around her head, calling a servant girl to bring her a hand mirror.

The young girl, who had been standing shyly in a corner, brought Madame Zebur a silver backed, hand mirror to admire her reflection in her new *hajab*. Janine was delighted that the elderly woman was pleased with the gift. And even more pleased when she ordered the young servant girl to show Janine around the upper rooms of the palace. This was just what Janine had been hoping for and it had seemed to come almost too easily. She protested that she had only a little time. But Madame Zebur assured her that it would not take long and that she would have a surprise waiting for her on her return.

The assurance made Janine a bit uneasy. She hoped that Amir was not in the house somewhere. It might be difficult trying to explain a second visit to his home uninvited. She followed the young girl around the upstairs balcony peering carefully into the upper bedrooms, each one more elaborate than the one before and all looking unused. The last room was a study, obviously a man's. The furniture was modern and there was a lap top computer open on the desk. Janine would have given a day of her life to access it. But she felt that she had pushed her luck about as far as it would go this morning and her hour was almost up. She wasn't sure that she would be lucky enough to locate another taxi outside the upper Casbah if her driver had decided to abandon her in favor of a better fare.

The girl led her back to Madame Zabur's rooms. The lovely old woman was still seated at her breakfast table, but she now had a jewelry box open on the table beside her. She smiled up at Janine as she entered. "What do you think of the house?" she asked proudly. "Do you agree that my grandson spoils me?"

"I do indeed. The rooms are lovely," Janine answered honestly. Even if they looked as though they were seldom used. Only the office showed signs of recent use and she was now eager to leave before Amir showed up unexpectedly. She wasn't sure what she had hoped to find out this morning. But so far it had only been a pleasant social visit accompanied by and excellent cup of French coffee.

Then Madame Zebur reached into her jewelry box and picked something out, holding it up to Janine. It was a simple gold bracelet that fit over the wrist without a clasp, like an ancient slave ornament. "I want you to have this as a reminder of our meeting." Madame Zebur said with a smile. "My grandson gives me so many gifts, that it is impossible to wear them all. As I rarely go out. He just brought this to me from Paris. I thought that it would look lovely on your arm."

Janine took the bracelet in her hand, shaking her head. " I can't accept something so expensive," she said honestly. "Besides your grandson might be angry if he knew that you gave it away," she continued, turning the rose gold ornament around to read the Arabic inscription inside. She held it to the light and read it again. It was obvious that Madame Zebur didn't read Arabic. The inscription said: 'to *my beloved sister Saroya from her brother, Said.*'

Chapter Seventeen

After saying her goodbye's hastily, Janine found the taxi waiting for her and made it back to the hotel in record time, with the bracelet safely in the pocket of her jeans. After reading the inscription, she couldn't leave it behind, even though she felt a certain sense of guilt accepting it from the elderly woman.

Rick was waiting for her in the lobby when she arrived. He was packed and ready to go and glowered at her as she breezed in. "Looking to be late for our departure," he growled.

"Packed and ready to go also," Janine said pulling the caftan over her head as she raced to the elevator. She patted her pocket as she ran, to reassure herself that the bracelet was still there. She wasn't sure what the connection was, but it was the first clue that she had found to Saroya's disappearance, and moreover that Amir was somehow connected to it. What the connection was she hadn't a clue. But he was either buying stolen property or he somehow was part of the disappearance of the Saudi Princess.

She was very silent on the plane, thinking through all the ramifications of her find, and wondering if she should somehow enlist Rick's help. He went back and forth to Algiers all the time and might have a way to find out more about Amir's business contacts. She broached the subject carefully over an excellent late lunch on the plane. Air France still fed its clients well. "What, if anything, do you know about Amir Zebur's business connections?" she asked casually.

"Is that what you have been ruminating about?" he said taking her hand casually.

She pulled it away, gently. "I have a reason to be curious."

"Well, so do we. From what I know, he is involved in most of the slightly risky but highly lucrative commerce that goes on in and out of Algeria." He signaled to the flight attendant to refill his drink. " Have you developed a crush on him?"

"Hardly," Janine answered, giving up her tray and asking for coffee. "He just strikes me as someone to watch."

"For your office or mine?" Rick continued slowly, cutting into an excellent piece of steak and offering some to Janine.

"Maybe for both of us. Have there ever been any rumors that connect him with al Qaida in North Africa?"

Rick put down his wine, looking even more serious. " Have you got something that I don't know about? Remember you are under contract to us for this visit."

Janine glanced at him, toying with the gold bracelet on her wrist. She had worn It for safety, not willing to put It into her luggage where it might just 'disappear'. "I may have something," she said smiling over at him. "I'll tell you about it after we get off the plane."

"Why not now?"

"If this is real, it is too fragile to talk about in public. Besides, I'm not sure yet what I am looking at," she said, smiling over at him. "Let's talk about something else until we land."

Later that evening, in the privacy of her own apartment, Janine took off the bracelet and translated the inscription again, carefully. She had been right the first time. It was Saroya's bracelet. She wished that she had been able to sneak a peek into Madame Zebur's jewelry box to see if any of the other items might have belonged to the Princess. She had caught a glimpse of an emerald and gold necklace, nestled in a bed of silk, that looked priceless. Was it possible that Amir had bought or stolen all of the Princess's jewels?

She put in a call to her office to see if anyone had a list of what had been taken from the hotel, or better yet photographs. A sleepy night-clerk told her that there might be something, but that Janine would have to wait till morning to find out. He was by himself and there was no way that he could access the file. Janine wheedled him, promising him a bottle of his favorite wine if he could locate a list or photos and send it to her encrypted this evening.

He wasn't in the mood to be helpful. But Janine was very insistent, even pulling a little rank which she never liked to do with the clerks. It didn't make working with them any easier. But she did get the file on her laptop later that evening. It was just a list of what the Saudi Embassy had reported stolen. There were no photographs, just a straight forward description and a monetary value. Janine shook her head in amazement. Young Saroya had been carrying around over two million dollars worth of jewelry, set with diamonds, emeralds and other precious stones. It had been uninsured and had disappeared from her hotel room presumably with her. That was all, and it was very little to work on. There was no mention of a gold bracelet, but a necklace set in gold and emeralds was one of the missing items. "Voila," Janine exclaimed to herself, more excited than she would care to admit.

She decided to take herself out for a late sandwich and a glass of wine at the local bistro, since as usual, there was nothing to eat in her tiny French fridge. If she had known who was lurking on the sidewalk outside her apartment. She might have decided to stay home.

The young Arab was in a foul mood. He had been standing in the cold outside the infidel's apartment every night for almost a week. No one had come in or out, until tonight, when at last there was a light upstairs in the apartment. He could see a shadow moving back and forth across the window. Perhaps tonight he would have the chance to strike for Allah and the cause of freedom. He felt the serrated blade in his pocket, running his finger carefully along its razor-sharp edge. He could imagine it cutting into her throat, as he attacked her from behind on the dark street. He would do it so fast that she wouldn't even have time to scream. Then he would leave her bleeding body there on the sidewalk as a warning to all the infidels who lived in this quarter.

He could hear the downstairs door opening. He pressed himself soundlessly against the wall in the shadows and waited. His breath came quickly. He could imagine himself doing the deed as he had so many times before. His breath came more rapidly. He had to clench the knife hard to keep his hands from shaking. He would not fail this time. His brothers could no longer taunt him for having failed to kill the woman the first time he was sent to do it. He stepped forward and raised his arm as the door opened. An elderly French couple stepped out in front of him. Before he could hide the knife, the man started shouting for the police and trying to push his portly wife back inside the doorway. She began to scream, but the man screamed louder, shoving his heavy body in front of her to protect her.

A shrill whistle pierced the evening, as a policeman came running to the scene. The Arab ran in the opposite direction, praying to Allah that he would not be caught. This was just a test of his resolution. Allah was trying to see how determined he was to kill the infidel. He ran a zig-zag course through the neighborhood and quickly reached the banks of the Seine, where he slowed and mingled with the tourists and the sightseers. He forced himself to walk slowly and not to look over his shoulder, a movement that would give him away, as would the knife in his pocket. He walked casually down the steps to the embankment, and reluctantly threw his precious knife into the rushing water. That way, if he should be caught and identified, he would not be carrying a weapon. The old Frenchman had looked him full in the face before he began screaming. That was not good. He could not stand another time in jail. He had to be free to kill the woman. His honor and the honor of his family demanded it.

Janine heard the noise downstairs. But she had taken time to change her clothes and put the bracelet into the small wall safe in her apartment. When she left the building, her neighbors were still being questioned by an earnest young policeman. They were outraged that such a crime had almost taken place in this fine old neighborhood. "What is France coming to?" the old man exclaimed. "We are becoming a country of thieves and murderers, no longer 'la belle France.'" The young policeman agreed soberly, taking down what he could of the statement in his notebook.

" But can you describe the man who almost attacked you, sir?" he kept asking.

He was rewarded with another angry outburst from the man and more sniffling from his wife. Finally the gentleman shouted in frustration. "All these rag-heads look alike. Why don't you just arrest them all? France and the neighborhood would be better for it." Then he ushered his wailing wife upstairs. Their outing for the evening spoiled.

Janine told the policeman what she knew, which wasn't much. But she had the feeling that whoever had frightened the elderly couple had probably been spying on her. She didn't like the feeling of being armed whenever she went out for a sandwich in the local bistro. But thinking better of it, she went back upstairs and got her Beretta. Then she strolled casually down Rue Belle Chasse toward the river. Just across from the Quay, there was a brightly lit cafe that served light snacks and stayed open late, serving the neighborhood and the waning tourist trade. She ordered hot tea and a smoked brie and ham sandwich, tucking into it hungrily while she considered her options.

She didn't know that a pair of angry eyes were eyeing her maliciously while she ate. The young Arab no longer had his knife, but he still had his hatred of the infidel. He stood in the shadows outside the café and watched her eat, memorizing her features. A policeman was coming down the street in front of him so he moved deeper into the shadows. As the policeman approached, the young man beat a hasty retreat. It would do no good to be caught now, while the woman still lived.

Janine felt a nervous tremor run through her body as she shrugged into her jacket. It wouldn't do to get antsy here in her own neighborhood. There had to be somewhere in the world that felt safe, and she had chosen her flat on Rue Belle Chasse for that reason. But something told her that the failed attack on the elderly couple had not been by chance this evening. The sooner she could get this assignment finished and be on to something else, the better.

But what did she have to go on? A bracelet that had probably belonged to a vanished princess with a very tenuous connection to a somewhat shady business man in Algiers, a man who lived in sumptuous style in a restored Palace in the Casbah. Who might know about him so that questioning them might not arouse too much suspicion? Certainly Unesco had representatives in Paris. Perhaps somewhere in their voluminous files there might be more information about the illusive Mr. Zebur and his restoration plans for his part of the Casbah. But whom did she know that might help her?

She pulled out her cell phone and called a friend at the Paris Herald Tribune. He didn't sound thrilled to be interrupted at dinnertime. Janine could hear children's voices in the room and the sound of music. She was tempted to contrast that with her lonely meal, but only for a moment. He gave her the name of someone he had interviewed recently at Unesco, and said that that she could use his name. "But she may not remember me," he said honestly. " I only interviewed her as background for the main story, and I didn't use the information that she gave me."

"All the better," Janine said gratefully, "I'll tell her that I am doing a follow up on your story."

"As long as you keep the Tribune out of this completely. But give me the story first if you find what you are looking for," he said, going back to his dinner.

" I'll stay in touch, don't worry." Janine said, noting down the woman's name on a napkin, while she finished her warm brie and ham. At least she had a lead for the morning. It was slim, but it was somewhere to start.

She walked home down the darkening street, her hand on her hip pocket where she had put the Beretta. It felt strange going to dinner armed in Paris. But someone considered her dangerous enough to want to have her frightened if not killed. She had been in situations like this before, lots of times, but never on her home turf. It made her angry at herself for being concerned and at the world for getting so dangerous. Who would have thought that she would have to be armed to walk alone down Rue Belle Chasse in the evening?

But she locked the downstairs door carefully as she went into the building and kept her gun in hand as she climbed the stairs. She opened the door to her apartment slowly and turned on the lights in all the rooms, checking the closets and under the bed and feeling almost foolish as she did so. But there was no point in taking chances. Especially when lives were at stake, possibly her own.

She awoke to a brisk fall morning with the sun shining brightly. The events of the night before seemed like a dream. She looked at her weapon on her bedside table and grimaced. Who would have thought that she would get to be such a Nervous Nelly? But she was clearly on to something, and whoever was out there didn't want her to go any further with her investigation. After two strong cups of French coffee and a rather stale croissant, she started calling the Unesco office. The woman that her friend had suggested she contact was not in. But the name got the receptionist's attention, so Janine took a chance and asked for the officer who was in charge of Unesco projects in Algeria.

After being asked the third time for her name and the purpose of her call, she was finally put through to a young woman who sounded annoyed at being bothered. Janine explained again that she had just returned from Algiers and had some questions that she would like to ask about the funding for their Casbah project.

This was met with a dead silence. Then the young woman again asked for her name.

Getting annoyed, Janine tried using the name that her newspaper friend had given her. "I was told to call her but it seems that she is not in today," she said in her best diplomatic voice, gritting her teeth. "I wonder if there is someone else that I might talk to about the Casbah restoration project?"

The young woman admitted that there was, but that Monsieur La Tour was not in yet. "Well, put me on his calendar for ten o'clock and leave a note on his desk that I am coming over to visit," Janine said pleasantly, and hung up before she could be told that it was too early or that the time slot was not available, or was asked one more time for her name.

She dressed carefully in what she considered appropriate for a major cultural institution, but she left the coat of her gray worsted suit open to accommodate her weapon. Then thinking better of it, she put it back in the drawer. She was sure to be scanned electronically and carrying a gun was probably not the best introduction to a UN office.

She found the address at 7 Place de Fontenoy on her map of Paris. It was near Napoleon's Tomb at Les Invalides and not too long a walk, if she cut through back streets. She liked Paris in the morning and it would avoid trying to hail a taxi in the rush hour. She cut over to Rue Saint Dominique and then to Boulevard des Invalides, tipping her mental hat to Napoleon as she strode by. In all the years that she had gone in and out of Paris, she had never bothered to go inside the marble mausoleum to see his tomb. It was curious that the French now found him such a hero. Time and history seemed to take the warts off all conquerors and politicians. She turned on to Avenue de Tournville and then, left to Avenue de Lowendal and found herself on Place de Fontenoy with minutes to spare. The building was somber and imposing, as benefited the center of the world's cultural preservation.

Janine sat on a bench outside for a moment to catch her breath, and plan her approach. Her excuse for being here was pretty thin. But she had to start somewhere to get information on Zebur's connection to the restoration project. She decided to play that card immediately, since it was really the only one that she had.

She was glad that she had left the Beretta at home as the security was unexpectedly thorough for a cultural agency. She stepped through a screening device and handed a guard her handbag, which he looked through carefully. He then nodded to her morosely and indicated that the office that she was looking for was upstairs. She scanned the list of office numbers and found La Tour's name at the end of the list and also at the end of the hall. Algeria must not be too high on the UN's list of priorities.

The door was unlocked, and there was no one in the office, not even a secretary. She took a seat in the one chair reserved for visitors and idly thumbed through a Unesco publication which was already a few years old. She scanned an article about the preservation of the Casbah. It seemed that from the beginning they had been short of cash. One of the problems was that the Algerians had not given the funds and services they had committed to the project. There were some glossy photos of palaces being restored on the outside. One of them even looked like the Zebur's villa. She wasn't sure, but at least it was a way to start the conversation, when and if La Tour arrived.

After about twenty minutes, when she was just about to give the interview up as a bad idea, the door was pushed open slowly and a dapper gentleman in a black suit, carrying a battered briefcase, came in and shut the door abruptly behind him. On seeing Janine, he burst into a flurry of rapid French, insisting loudly that she must be in the wrong office. He had no appointments this morning.

Armed with this information. Janine became her most charming. She apologized for coming without a formal appointment. She knew what a busy man he was, she said with a straight face. But she had called and asked an uncooperative secretary to put a note on his desk requesting an appointment. "I am an acquaintance of Madame Zebur, who kindly invited me to tour her marvelous palace in the Casbah." she finished calmly, not moving from her seat, though La Tour had given no indication that he was inviting her to stay.

" It is such a shame that the funds to complete the project are not available," Janine continued innocently. " It is such an important project."

"Who told you that we were lacking funds?" the man huffed arrogantly, straightening his impeccable desk calendar.

"It says that right here in your own publication," Janine answered sympathetically, waving the Unesco magazine in his face.

The Frenchman seemed taken aback. He quickly sat down at his desk and began rifling through his briefcase for some papers. Not finding what he wanted immediately, he glared at Janine. "Why have you come here with these questions, Madame?" he inquired stiffly. "Do you have some official connection with the restoration project?"

"No, only a curiosity about a friend's home, which I admire greatly. I have just returned from Algiers where Madame Zebur was very kind to me."

"Then you must know that we are doing everything possible to complete the restoration of her villa, and of all the villas on the upper level, as I'm sure you noticed." He folded his hands across his comfortable middle and leaned back in his chair, his glance daring Janine to continue her questions.

Since she had never been able to resist a dare, Janine continued in a reasonable voice, taking a risk. " But surely Monsieur Zebur's generous contributions have helped?"

The Frenchman seemed to grow larger in his chair, glaring at Janine. "Who contributes to our projects, in what amount and for what purpose is none of your business.

Madame," he said, almost spitting at her in his anger. "Monsieur Zebur's contributions are his own affair." Janine had the feeling that if she hadn't been taller than he, he would have attempted to throw her bodily out of his office. He was now standing behind his desk, looking ready to say something that he might later regret.

Janine decided that it was time to exit gracefully. She had the clue that she had come for. Zebur was contributing heavily to the restoration of his portion of the Casbah. Now the only thing left to find out was where his money was coming from. A computer search might prove useful, and she knew someone who could do it for her, if she could talk him into it.

Chapter Eighteen

Sam was not amused when she asked him for the favor. " You want me to do what?" he hissed. " Don't you have fellas in your department who have higher clearance than I do in my retirement?"

"Yes, but they are not as sneaky as you are." Janine answered, flattering her old friend. "Besides I don't want the boys to know what tack I'm on, till I see if it pans out or not. This whole situation is rather iffy. I just want to know what his legitimate businesses are and how much he contributed to the Unesco last year. Can't you just look up his tax returns?"

"If he filed them. Algerian law might be a lot different from ours," Sam huffed.

"But he also holds French citizenship. He is very proud of that since his grandmother was French. He might have declared those contributions in France."

"Boy, you are really into this deep." Sam said jokingly. "Are you sure that you want me to find all this out? Is he a prospective suitor?"

"Not in this life," Janine said firmly. "Just get what you can on him and I'll owe you a great dinner."

"My place or yours?"

"Just great cous cous, in a local place I know. As you are aware, I can't and don't cook," Janine said, ignoring his invitation, as she had for years. He was too good a friend to turn into a date.

"Your loss," Sam said. grinning mischievously into the telephone. "I'll call you as soon as I have anything. I have to query my sources."

He called her back later in the day on her cell phone. " I'm not sure how much you really want to know about this guy. He has lots of irons in the fire, most of them more or less legal. The only thing of real interest that I turned up is a strong connection to the Saudi royal family."

"Bingo," Janine whispered, all sorts of possible connections vying for place in her head.

"Sam, you are on for dinner tonight. You pick the place."

"Cous Cous sounds great," he answered benignly. "I may have found some more tidbits that I can share over dinner."

"Do you mind if I invite a friend."

"Not as long as she is as pretty as you are."

Janine didn't answer. She hadn't seen Rick since they returned from Algiers. She wondered how he and Sam would get along after so many years, and what plan they could all come up with by sharing their expertise.

Butting their heads together might be more like it, Janine thought as the two men arrived almost at the same time, both thinking that they had earned the right to her undivided attention. Rick looked fit and tanned after the trip to Algiers and Sam was as rumpled as usual. But after circling each other for a few minutes like two rutting stags, they shook hands and seemed genuinely glad to see each other.

Janine ordered, since it was her party, and she knew what the best dishes were that were served here. The men didn't seem to mind as long as she let Sam order the wine. He considered himself a connoisseur and took a long time choosing from the limited wine card. This was, after all, a Tunisian café and catered to a non-drinking clientele.

As the cous cous was served, Janine broached the subject of the evening: Her investigation of Zebur and the fact that she now had Princess Saroya's bracelet in the safe in her apartment, a gift from his grandmother.

"That doesn't surprise me at all," Sam said, taking a sip of his favorite German white wine. "The man is involved with the Saudi's in a number of business deals. Saudi money is funding most of his projects in Algiers, and elsewhere."

Rick looked interested. "They've been sniffing around our project too. They have so many petrodollars to spend they don't know where to stop investing. So far our company is sticking with Algerian money, but if these costs overrides continue, due to increased security, we will be taking any legitimate funding that comes our way."

"And some not so legitimate?" Janine asked, as she tasted a succulent *brique*, spicy meat and egg in a crisp pastry, her favorite hors d'ouevre.

"That too," Sam answered, pouring himself another glass of wine. "From what I found out this afternoon, this guy has his fingers in a lot of pies. He also has contributed very generously to the Casbah renewal project. Just recently more than one million dollars."

" How did you find that out?" Rick grinned.

"His donations are in the public records if you know where to look." Sam answered smugly, tucking into his *Tangine,* with a bland look on his pudgy face.

"But where does he get that kind of money to give away?" Janine mused.

"Maybe he did a big favor for the Saudis," Rick answered, smiling at Janine. "Maybe he made a problem that they were dealing with, or an embarrassment, go away."

" Princess Saroya, or her jewelry, worth about two million, give or take a necklace or two," Janine answered, too excited to finish her meal. "But how do we prove any of this?"

"With great difficulty," Rick said, wiping his mouth and ordering a cup of mint tea to finish his meal. "We have means and motive, but the method is not immediately apparent."

"Unless he happens to know Prince Said," Janine answered. "If we can connect those two, then maybe he was doing his friend a favor to make his troublesome sister just disappear."

"And keep her jewels for the favor," Rick added. " Not a bad trade off."

"But how do we prove it?"

"We don't prove anything," Rick answered grimly "This flies right in the face of my company's Algerian project. If we start making false accusations about one of their leading citizens, the whole thing could go up in smoke. You know how touchy the Arabs are. They may not like or trust one another but they tend to band together when attacked from the outside." He rose to his feet to go. "Count me out of this one, Janine, and please don't use my company's name in your investigations."

"That's going to be a bit hard to do, since I was in Algeria at their invitation." Janine answered smartly, reaching for the bill over Sam's protestations.

"My treat, since I don't cook," she said slapping his hand and putting down her credit card.

"When shall we three meet again" Sam said, quoting Shakespeare's Macbeth, as he finished the last drop of wine in his glass.

Rick did not look amused. " I told you that I am sitting this one out. If you two want to try to track down what happened to Saroya, please keep my company's name of it. I want to retire after this project and I don't expect to be broke."

"Oh, broke isn't too bad," Sam said jokingly as he rose from the table. "Take it from a retired army officer. Things could be worse. You obviously have to take this to your boss," Sam added to Janine. "The Saudi's have asked for help from us and also from the French. Withholding any evidence, no matter how tenuous, is not an option."

Janine agreed. But she knew that as soon as she went to the big boys with the evidence, her hands would probably be tied. But it was a move that she had to make sooner rather than later.

****

The meeting went rather as she suspected it would. The 'boys' were interested that she had the bracelet, but they didn't see it as conclusive evidence that Zebur had had anything to do with Saroya's disappearance. However, they were glad to have something to share with the Saudis to show that they were still on the case as requested. The French hadn't turned up anything yet, so it put the US office a bit ahead of the game. It was a position that they relished as the French Security National liked to play one upmanship at every opportunity. Her boss essentially told Janine to keep working on the case but to stay quiet about the bracelet and where she had gotten it. Zebur was put on a list to keep an eye on. But that was about all.

Janine left the meeting feeling puzzled. Clearly there was something else going on that she was not party to. She was out in the cold again and being told essentially to solve the problem on her own. Actually, that was her favorite place to be, in a way she was glad of the office reaction. It meant that they would stay out of her way and give her a chance to work on her own. It was a position that she rather liked, even if it left her without many official resources.

It was difficult to turn up any more information on her own about Zebur, beyond what Sam had already given her, so she decided to try another tack. She decided to call the Minister's office and ask for an appointment with Jalila. It was possible that Jalila could give her a lead to other contacts in the French/Algerian community who might know about Zebur's business associates. It was a close-knit community, especially among the successful émigrés. It was possible that Jalila had heard something or knew someone who might have information. It was a long shot, but it was worth a try.

Janine called the Minister's office and was pleased that Jalila took the call right away. In her throaty voice, Jalila said that she was delighted to hear from Janine and would be happy to see her in her office the following morning. When she asked what the meeting was about, Janine answered that it was a 'personal matter.' It was a phrase that kept the door open but didn't reveal much. Which was just what Janine intended. If she had to pretend a possible romantic interest in Zebur, so be it.

Jalila received her in a very functional office in the Ministry of Urban affairs. She was dressed in her usual gray suit but today with a scarlet blouse and her thick auburn hair swept back from her face. She had a slightly worried look, but Janine decided that her expression was generic. Her desk was piled high with paper work and for a minute Janine felt somewhat guilty about imposing on their slight friendship.

But Jalila seemed genuily delighted to see her and invited Janine to sit by the window and join her in a cup of sweet Arab tea. "I learned to enjoy this in Tunisia," Janine said, as she accepted the fragile cup, inhaling its spicy aroma.

"What brings you to see me?" Jalila asked, leaning forward, and getting straight to the heart of the matter. "What is this 'personal matter' of which you spoke?"

Janine decided to be a frank as possible without giving away everything. " It concerns Amir Zebur. I need to know more about his activities here in France. They are difficult to track down, and I thought that you might have run across some information about him among your colleagues."

Jalila looked thoughtful, sipping her tea. Then she said quietly, " Is this for personal or professional reasons?"

"A little of both," Janine lied, implying an interest that she did not feel.

"Well, then you know that he is married," Jalila answered politely. "He does not live with his wife all the time. Madame Zebur is French and lives here in Paris. I believe that they are business partners." she said thoughtfully. "They have investments in some of the housing projects that my office oversees. That is all the information that I have about him," she said, putting down her cup and brushing some crumbs off her lap. " I would not advise you to get involved with him. I have heard that he can become violent when angry."

Just then the telephone rang loudly, and looking somewhat annoyed, Jalila arose to answer it. She held a conversation in rapid French with the person on the other end of the line. When she hung up she made her apologies to Janine. " I'm afraid that I must attend an important meeting," she smiled apologetically. "If I can be of any further assistance in your 'personal matter' please call me. I enjoyed our time in Algeria together and would like to know you better when there is time. But in the meantime, if you would like my advice, I would give Monsieur Zebur a wide berth. He is what you Americans call 'bad news,' she said, smiling at her use of American slang.

Chapter Nineteen

So Amir had a wife in Paris who was his business partner, but whom he didn't live with. That was interesting information. Janine pondered it on the way home on the crowded Metro. In Algeria he certainly behaved like a bachelor, while his French wife, it could be assumed, looked after their business interests in Paris. Janine wondered if she was in on whatever schemes he was involved in, or if she was just and innocent bystander with a husband who cheated on her at every opportunity.

There were a number of Zeburs listed in the telephone directory. Janine finally had to call on Sam's help again to find the right one. It seemed that Madame was a well- known dress designer for the very affluent. She had a salon in an exclusive part of Paris near the Champs Elysees. Here she welcomed the wives of the rich and famous, but especially the wives of oil rich Arabs visiting Paris to buy outfits that they could only wear under their *abayas* or at home. It was the kind of salon that Princess Saroya might have frequented. Certainly it was in her price range.

Janine dressed carefully for the visit. But there was little in her wardrobe that could disguise her as a wealthy Arab. So she decided to go deliberately casual. She put on jeans and a black cashmere sweater and scarf and her best gold earrings. A black leather jacket and shoulder bag held her Beretta and her cell phone. So she was well equipped for the chase. She called first to make sure that Madame was in, pretending to be an American who was with a film company shooting in France. Using the name of a movie star whom she had heard was in town, got her an appointment to view the collection that afternoon.

The boutique was discrete despite its location in the center of Paris. A black lacquered door held a simple gold sign indicating that it was 'Madame Zebur's Collection'. The bell chimed discretely when she pressed it. A gray haired woman wearing a neat black and white maid's uniform opened the door. Janine could hear the subtle whine of Arab music coming from the rear of the building. The foyer was furnished with gold and brocade furniture, clustered around oval white rugs, on shiny black floors. Long mirrors adorned the walls, and the room was filled with the scent of attar of rose perfume.

The maid, after taking Janine's black leather jacket, ushered her into the back of a long room where the guests for the showing of the current collection were seated. Janine was grateful that the lights were very dim as she slithered into a gilded chair at the rear of the audience. The room was filled with well groomed and bejeweled women, many of them in *abaayas* covering them completely. A few women were wearing head-scarves pulled down tightly to the top of their eyebrows. It was certainly an eclectic group of customers.

It was immediately clear who was in charge. Madame Zebur was a large woman, hiding her fat behind flowing robes. Her chubby hands glittered with a bouquet of brightly colored rings, flashing semiprecious stones. She held a microphone to her lips like a pop singer and began to describe what the models were wearing, first in French and then in fluent Arabic. The clothes were in primary colors, smartly tailored and suitable for life in Paris. There was a smattering of applause as the models preened and turned, all of them looking anorexic. But there was a whispering among the Arab women and an air of excitement about what was to come.

The reason was soon clear. The music changed to the crooning sounds of Oum Kaltoum, the famous Arab popular singer of love songs. A trio of models came out dressed in the traditional *abaayas*, long shapeless shrouds with high necks and wide sleeves that covered every inch of their arms and most of their hands. The robes were in gray, bronze and black. Fashioned of a kind of silky material, that never the less showed nothing of the models figures. The dresses easily could have been shown on coat hangers instead of on beautiful Parisian models.

Then a curious thing happened. As they pranced and turned, the models, one after another began a kind of smiling striptease. First one and then another peeled off their long sleeves, revealing their milky white arms and necks covered with sparkling jewels. They fashioned the sleeves into belts with a curious twist, which outlined their hips and waists. There was a gasp of admiration among the Arab women and bursts of laughter. Then with a final burst of music from Oum Kaltoum, the models unzipped the side of their *abaayas* to reveal most of their slender legs and their feet attired in spike heel, strap sandals. More appreciative laughter and clapping came from the audience.

As her finale, Madame Zebur stepped into the spotlight surrounded by the models in their transformed gowns and accepted the enthusiastic applause of her entirely female audience. Her round forehead was covered with beads of perspiration, but her face wore a look of triumph. She had discovered a way for traditional Arab women to please both themselves and their husbands. And she was going to make a fortune in the process.

When the lights came up slowly in the room. Janine looked at her program and was astonished at the prices. But the women were flocking to place their orders with a lovely young woman sitting at a small table at the far side of the room. She was dressed entirely in black and had long silky hair hanging almost to her waist. She looked like a younger and slimmer Madame Zebur. And Janine surmised that she might be her daughter. A tantalizing display of jeweled evening bags and beaded scarves were on the table beside her. This gave the women another chance to shop for accessories while placing their orders. What ever else she was, Madame Zebur was a smart marketer.

Janine slid over as unobtrusively as possible to hear what the Arab women were ordering and if possible to catch their names. It wasn't difficult since they seemed to be trying to outdo one another in placing orders. The young woman had a satisfied smile on her face as she wrote down descriptions of what each woman wanted. The convertible *abaayas* were obviously a big hit, but so were some of the more traditional evening clothes and dinner dresses. Janine sidled over to the tea table, trying to keep a low profile.

But Madame Zebur had been tracking her with wary eyes. When the show was over, and before Janine could slip out the door, Madame Zebur accosted her with questions about the star whose name Janine had mentioned to wangle an invitation to the event. "Well, we are not really friends," Janine admitted honestly, since she didn't know the woman at all. "But I have heard so much about your work as a couturier, that I admit that I used her name to get a chance to see your collection."

"Do you often wear couturier clothing?" Madame Zebur purred looking Janine up and down critically.

"Not in my line of work" Janine answered frankly, and was pleased to see the other woman's startled look.

"And what line of work might that be?" the woman asked suspiciously.

"I am an investigator looking into the disappearance of Princess Saroya," Janine said, taking a chance on the effect of candor. "I understand that she was one of your clients. What can you tell me about her?"

Madame Zebur's eyes narrowed. She was about to say something, then thought better of it. She smiled over Janine's head at one of her clients who was leaving, her arms filled with packages wrapped in gold and pink tissue paper. "Wait for a few moments and we can talk if you like," she hissed, before she followed the client to the door, talking and smiling

The young woman in black walked over to Janine, carrying a large notebook. "Do you wish to place and order?" she said politely, taking in Janine's casual attire.

Janine smiled. "I would love to try one of those convertible *abayas, to* surprise some of the Arab men I know."

"You would be certain to please them," the young woman said charmingly. Then she smiled professionally. "We are finding that they are very popular; they serve a multitude of uses in a more traditional society, the woman can be modest in the world."

"And immodest at home," Janine continued for her. "Very practical, if expensive."

" Expense is rarely and issue for our clients", the young woman said, smiling.

" No, I can see it wouldn't be" Janine answered, watching a cluster of women leave in a group, all with servants following them, laden with packages.

"Perhaps you would like to try something on," the young woman insisted, indicating several dressing rooms at the end of the salon.

When Janine hesitated again, the young woman took her arm firmly and, smiling in her mother's direction, led Janine to the rear of the room, which was slowly emptying of clients. "You are looking for Saroya," she whispered, barely moving her lips. "I also wish to find her, if she is still alive. She was my friend and came here often. I have not heard anything from her for several weeks." She pulled a dress off one of the open racks and, holding it up in front of herself, almost pushed Janine into an open dressing room.

When they were both inside, she made a great display of taking the dress off the hanger and holding it up in front of Janine, "My mother doesn't know that Saroya and I were such good friends," she whispered. "Mother saw her as only a very wealthy client. But the Princess told me many things about her life, things that I could not tell my mother. She was planning to run away to America to marry an architect she met in Paris. The day after she told me about her secret romance, she disappeared."

Janine resisted taking off her clothes to try on the elegant dress. She didn't need to go any further to establish a contact between Saroya and the Zeburs. "Did your father or mother know of your friendship?" Janine asked quietly, reluctantly fingering the rich material of the dress she had refused to try on.

The girl looked surprised. " What do you know about my family? Do you know my father?" she asked suspiciously.

"Only by reputation," Janine parried. "But I was fortunate enough to meet your grandmother when I was in Algiers recently."

The girl smiled, lighting up her lovely face. " My Omar is very dear to me," she said quietly, " Is she well?"

Janine resisted getting into a discussion of family matters. "Can you give me the date when Saroya was last here?"

The young woman looked troubled. Then her face brightened as she opened the large black ledger that she was still carrying. "I may have the date here," she said softly. "She bought many things to add to her trousseau, but she never sent for them. A servant came to pay for them, but they were never picked up. That is what made me suspicious that something had happened to her," she said, frowning and showing Janine the entry in her ledger.

The amount that the Princess had spent in one day would have bought Janine clothes for five years. But she tried not to look surprised. The date was the day before the Princess had disappeared from the Ritz hotel. The clothes had been paid for three days later, but never picked up.

"What will you do with her things, if no one comes to claim them?" Janine asked softly.

"My mother will sell them again. She has no conscience," the young woman answered bitterly. " She did not like Saroya at all. Even though she spent a great deal of money here. She thought that she was spoiled and pampered beyond belief. She thinks that she got what was coming to her," the girl blurted out suddenly.

"And what was that?" Janine asked kindly.

The girl looked frightened, her face white and her voice barely above a whisper. "Whatever it is, it is the worst that her brother can do to her. But I think that my mother knows. She has some of her jewels. You saw part of them today on the models. That wasn't paste they were wearing. It was the real thing. That is what frightens me most of all. The fact that whatever happened, our business profited from it in some way. I can't rest until I know what happened to my friend. Can you help me?"

Chapter Twenty

Janine took her name, Sari. And her cell phone number and promised to call her if she had any information about Saroya. She again asked if the jewels were real and if her mother didn't fear detection by having her models wear them. Sari grimaced. "She has no shame," she whispered. " She thinks that it serves Saroya right to have her fabulous jewelry worn by paid models. She was angry with her because she thought that my father had eyes for her."

"And did he?" Janine asked, pushing her luck a little further.

The girl looked ashamed. "It is possible. As you can see, my mother is no longer young and she is angry with him. He does not often visit her anymore." She busied herself tying up some packages, all the while looking out for her mother to return and catch her talking with Janine..

When Madame did come over to the changing booth, it was like a cruise ship parting the seas. The servants and sales girls who were still in the room stepped back as though for the queen of England. "Has my daughter shown you something to your liking?" Madame asked in a voice that carried across the room. " If not, perhaps you would like to return at a later time. The showing is over," she said, taking Janine's arm and almost pulling her toward the door.

Janine let her self be led, or almost pushed. She admired the woman's moxie. To have the guts to show her designer line with Saroya's jewels as accessories, when half the police in Paris were looking for them and for Saroya, took a lot if guts.

She wondered if Madame Zebur's daughter was telling the truth. She really had no reason to lie that Janine could think of. But knowing that the jewelry was in Madam Zebur's possession didn't make her job any easier. It just gave her one more clue in the curious puzzle that surrounded the Princess's disappearance from the Ritz Hotel.

Since it was almost evening, Janine decided to back track to the Ritz in the chance that there would be another attendant at the desk. She had gotten a cold shoulder from the first one, and little or no information. Perhaps taking another tack would give her an additional lead. Besides, she liked the grand old hotel with its aura of another more genteel age. It was the favorite hangout of the Saudi royalty, particularly of the married ones. It was safe place to stash a young wife or wives, while the males did the town unencumbered.

Since it was getting late, Janine took a taxi, holding her breath as the taxi drove like he was following an ambulance. He deposited her at the main door, telling her that she was his last fare of the day and looking disdainfully at his tip. Janine ignored him. He probably made more money in a day than she did anyhow. And she had already overspent her advance for this case, such as it was.

The lobby of the hotel was almost deserted at this hour. It was too late for cocktails and early for dinner and most of the guests had already checked in or out. The desk attendant was new, but no more helpful than the first one had been. He deliberately turned aside all of Janine's questions about the coming and goings of Saudi royalty. "There will be a representative here from the Saudi Embassy later in the evening for the reception," he said haughtily, "Perhaps you can address any legitimate questions to him."

'Hmm,' Janine thought, a Saudi reception later this evening. There was sure to be a crowd. One that she might pass unnoticed in if she could just get inside the banquet room which she could see was being readied, through a half opened door, as waiters sauntered in and out carrying covered silver trays.

There was no chance that she could pass as a guest, dressed as she was. She regretted not taking one of Madame Zebur's outfits, and returning it later. As she knew certainly that some well-heeled clients occasionally did. But she was stuck here in her working clothes and that didn't bode well for crashing the party. She strolled into the bar, which was dark and almost deserted at this hour of the evening. She ordered a tonic water and sat at the polished bar, sipping it slowly while she thought about how to crash the Saudi reception.

A man and woman, who looked vaguely familiar, came into the bar. They were dressed as casually as Janine and speaking French. She gathered by their conversation that they were from the newspaper Le Monde and that the man was scheduled to cover the reception for his paper that evening. It sounded as though the woman had made other plans and was insisting that he come to the theater with her instead. They weren't exactly fighting, but their voices were loud enough so that Janine could follow their conversation in the almost empty room.

Finally the man agreed to go with his friend to the theater and to come back to the reception during the intermission. "Not much happens at these things anyhow," he said, by way of excusing himself. "Just a bunch of Saudi princelings trying to outdo one another with their solid gold watches and diamond cuff links."

The woman whispered something in his ear that made him laugh and pat her on her round bottom, encased in slim jeans. "I'll pick up my pass at the door when I come back," he said teasingly. "I don't want to misplace it at the theater," he continued archly, looking down at her opulent breasts, prominently outlined in a low cut silk blouse.

Janine finished her drink and then went to the powder room to comb her short hair and put on some earrings. With her leather jacket belted tight and her high- heeled black boots, she hoped that she could pass for a reporter for Le Monde. With luck she could get in and get a quick look at Saroya's brother. Perhaps even ask him a question or two before they threw her out as an imposter. It was worth a try. Besides she liked the idea of crashing a Saudi Royal event. It was something she hadn't ever tried so do. And she liked new experiences, she told herself.

She hung out in the bar until the party was in full swing. There was a table near the door with press badges and a large *throb*, red and black checkered headdress wearing Saudi in charge, looking over the press corps carefully as they picked up their badges. Again Janine was glad that she had left her Beretta at home. She could see that the Le Monde badge was one of the few left on the table. Most of the press corps seemed younger than usual, and only a few of them were women, a bow to Saudi ingrained suspicion of the female sex.

Janine picked up the remaining badge and strode through the door, uttering a greeting in Arabic to the guardian of the press passes. He was so taken aback that he didn't react till she was through the door. Janine made sure that she was well across the room and mingling with the large crowd before he could stop her to ask to see her credentials.

The men were almost undistinguishable from one another. Many of them wore the long white robe and the red checkered headdress of the Saudi aristocracy. The rest of the men were in business suits. The few women were mostly European and dressed in expensive cocktail dresses with lavish jewelry. Platters of hors d'oeuvres and fruit juice were being passed and Arabic music blared from a concealed stereo system. Janine saw only a few people who were dressed as casually as she was and she took care to avoid them.

She accepted a glass of fruit juice from a passing waiter, who ogled her informal outfit. Janine gave him a death stare and started to move casually around the outskirts of the room. She could overhear snatches of Arabic conversation as well as French and some English. It seemed as though a number of deals were being confirmed with the swigging of fruit juice by the numerous Saudi guests. Janine didn't know what she really hoped to accomplish besides the obvious pleasure of crashing the party, when she heard someone calling her name.

She turned around to see Amir Zebur standing in back of her looking at her in amusement. "We seem to meet in the strangest places, Mademoiselle" he said, looking her up and down. " How did you come to be at this party? Don't tell me that you have a personal invitation from a Saudi prince?" he asked maliciously.

Janine decided to tell the truth. "Not at all," she said honestly. "I had hoped to meet Prince Said. I have heard so much about him."

Amir looked her up and down carefully, examining every detail of her outfit. "If you will excuse me for saying so, *ma cherie,* you are not exactly his type. He goes for much younger and more elegantly dressed women."

Janine refused to be put off by his comments. She had long since stopped being sensitive about her age and unmarried status. Let Amir believe what he wanted to. The main thing was to get him to introduce her to prince Said. She smiled knowingly. " He may be interested in knowing that I might have information about the location of his sister's jewels."

Amir smiled carefully, looking around and then pulling her to the edge of the room. "What do you know about these things," he hissed. " Who are you really and who are you working for?"

Janine knew that she had him caught, if only for the moment. "I work for myself," she said casually, playing him along. "You can think of me as a sort of a bounty hunter. I like to locate expensive things that are lost."

"And you get paid for this?" he snarled.

"In a manner of speaking. Sometimes just finding them is enough of a reward," she answered charmingly.

Just then, they were approached by a group of young Saudis. They eyed Janine for a moment and then ignored her as they began to talk with Amir in their guttural Arabic. Janine could understand enough of the conversation to know that it was about some kind of oil deal with Algeria. It seemed that Amir had his fingers in a number of pies. He tried to move the group away from Janine, but she stuck like butter on toast. This was more than she had bargained for. She wasn't sure that Amir knew she could understand most of the conversation. But her presence in the room was obviously making him very uncomfortable. "If you will introduce me to the prince, I will leave you in peace." She whispered seductively in Amir's ear, before moving slightly away form the group.

He took her arm and pushed her toward the door. "Please leave before I have to call security and embarrass you," he said grimly. "You have no right to be at this reception. It is a closed affair."

"Oh, but I represent the press tonight" Janine said, flashing her press pass quickly and then putting it back in her pocket. "I have every right to be here. I was assured that there was a story."

"The only story will be when I throw you forcefully out of the room," he snarled.

"Or even better, turn you over to the security police as an intruder."

Janine pulled away from him smilingly, as though he had just made a charming remark. Her eye was caught by an amazingly handsome young Saudi, the image of the Princess who had disappeared, advancing toward them.

The young man greeted Amir affectionately kissing him on both cheeks in the Saudi manner and ignoring Janine as though she were a piece of furniture. He put his arm around Amir and began to talk into his ear and lead him towards the center of the room to an animated group of young Saudis.

Janine was dumbstruck. She hadn't realized that Princess Saroya and her brother were twins. The resemblance was amazing. The young man even moved with feminine grace as he held on to Amir as though he were a long lost brother. Clearly he and the Algerian had more than a passing acquaintance. This made Amir's possession of some of the missing Princess's jewelry even more suspicious.

Janine saw Amir nod to a security guard, and gesture in her direction. She didn't need a stronger hint. She made her way rapidly toward the door nodding and smiling as though she knew some of the guests. When she got to the entrance she took off her press pass and left it on the table under the eyes of an astonished security guard. Then she quickly vanished into a nearby lady's room and counted to one hundred before she emerged, and sauntered toward the hotel exit. The evening hadn't been a waste after all. Now she just had to find a reasonable pattern for the facts that she had accumulated this afternoon and evening and put them together into a reasonable scenario.

As she hailed a taxi, she saw the real reporter for Le Monde emerge from another one and hurry into the hotel. She felt like telling him that she had been keeping his badge warm for him, while he had been keeping his girlfriend warm instead. But she decided to keep her smart remarks to herself for once. Perhaps that could be counted as personal progress.

Chapter Twenty One

On the way home in the taxi, she kept puzzling over the astonishing resemblance between the vanished Princess and her brother. It was uncanny. The young man even moved with a feminine grace, which was not unusual in the Saudi aristocracy. Then there was his obvious attachment to Amir and the fact that Amir's wife was using some of Saroya's jewels to decorate her models. There was a close connection that had to be examined, but where to take the next step? She had made herself a pariah in the Saudi society by crashing their party tonight. If Amir had told them who she was pretending to be, she was surely on their black list now. There had to be some other avenue to take in her search for the truth. But what was it? How to get behind the locked and bolted door of Saudi society to find the answers?

The Embassy sometimes kept records of the coming and going's of people who were involved in a case. Certainly now when they had been asked to help with the search for the Princess, records might exist of when the Prince and his followers had arrived in Paris, and where they were staying. They might also know if a Saudi plane had left Paris immediately after the princess had disappeared. It was worth a try. And she certainly didn't have anything else to do with the rest of her evening, her social life, or lack of it, being what it was.

The Embassy was formally closed for the evening, but it was guarded by a bored young Marine captain, who was glad for a few minutes distraction. After chatting him up for a few minutes, and showing him her credentials, he agreed to call the records room to see if anyone was still working there this late. It turned out that she was in luck and after again carefully checking her credentials, he agreed to let her go down and talk to the one person who was still on duty. " I don't know what you are looking for but most of what we work in here is classified," he said in a lilting voice, with overtones of Louisiana.

"I'm working on something that involves the Embassy" Janine shared casually. "I just need to check the Air Attaché's records for a flight out of Paris. "Nothing unusual," she continued, smiling at him as he buzzed her through the secure entrance.

The sandy haired young man who got to his feet to welcome her from an inner office, looked as through he had been taking a nap. His shirt was unbuttoned at the neck and he was less than delighted to be disturbed this late in the evening. But after examining Janine's credentials, he became less surly. He asked her to follow him down a dimly lit hall to where the computer center was lodged in the basement of the building. There were a few other bored looking clerks still on duty. They looked up as the pair entered; seeming to be pleased at any interruption of what must be uninteresting night duty.

"Just exactly what do you need?" The clerk asked in a languid French voice.

"Nothing much," Janine answered him in French. "I'm just checking on the departure of a private Saudi plane on or around these dates." And she gave him the date on which Saroya had been taken from the Ritz hotel. He looked at her curiously. But he was too well trained to ask questions. This sort of request came continually, and through their special computer network, the information was not difficult to find. Every plane leaving France had to be logged in to the French air control. He played with his keyboard for a few minutes while lights flashed and he shook his head several times, muttering to himself. Finally he turned to Janine and gave her a Gallic shrug of his shoulders.

"Several private Saudi planes were logged in arriving on and around that date. But none left any of the Paris airports, or the ones on the outskirts of the city. Is it possible that the people you are looking for left from another city?"

"Not likely," Janine muttered, thanking him and heading for the hallway. If Saroya hadn't left by plane, then she or her dead body were still in Paris. And her brother Prince Said knew where she was. It was impossible to get to Saudi Arabia from Paris by train or camel caravan. So the Princess had probably never left France, unless her body was somewhere at the harbor in Marseilles. That narrowed the search down by about a thousand or so miles. Why didn't this information make her feel any closer to a solution?

She stopped in her favorite bistro on the way home to think the situation over. The Princess. couldn't have simply disappeared, she was too closely monitored by her brother and his black suited 'minders.' Whatever had happened to her, her brother had to be involved in it. A strange thought crossed her mind and then she quickly pushed it away as being too illogical. Amir's closeness to the Princess's brother and the fact that his wife not only had her jewels, but was displaying them in public, continued to trouble her. What was the connection? Was the Prince paying Amir off for some services? Possibly getting rid of his twin sister, who had compromised the family's honor by her wild behavior?

She took a sip of her drink and continued to gaze out the window into the darkened street. She could see her reflection in the glass. Her hair was wild and she looked tired. It now took longer for her to recover from late nights. Sometimes she thought about what she would do when her career with the agency was over. She had lived on an adrenaline high for so many years, that she wasn't sure that she would know how to exist in the 'real' world, a world that didn't present daily puzzles to be solved, and the rush of success when she finally figured things out.

She wasn't sure that a quiet life in her Paris apartment would suit her completely. What would she do after she had visited all the art galleries she now didn't have time for? She shivered, and stood up to leave. A movement just outside the window caught her eye. He was there again, the same young Arab who had been following her the other evening.

She stood up, buttoning her coat; she went out to face the enemy head on.

*****

Rick hadn't heard from Janine since they returned from Algiers. He had rung her at home several times and left messages on her cell phone, but she had not returned his calls. For some reason he had begun to worry about her, and he was disgusted with himself for doing so. 'She's a tough cookie and can take care of herself,' his inner voice kept telling him. But another more persistent voice caused him to be concerned. That voice convinced him that it would be a good idea to drop by her flat just to get the lay of the land. It was a clear night so he decided to jog over, combining exercise with a nagging concern for her security.

They practically collided just outside her building. She was walking rapidly with her head down taking giant strides as though she was chasing something. Rick grabbed by the arms and she turned to hit him where it would hurt most. "Don't ever grab me like that again," she hissed. "You might get what I had ready for the guy who has been following me from the bistro."

"What guy?" Rick asked, looking around warily.

"Some Arab kid who is trying to make a name for himself by hassling me."

"So I guess it was a good idea that I showed up."

"If you think so," Janine answered, patting the pocket of her coat, where her Beretta should have been, if she hadn't left it behind to visit the Embassy. "Come on upstairs for a minute and let me share a puzzle with you. I could use some help in figuring this one out."

Surprised to be invited in to her inner sanctum, Rick agreed quickly. He insisted on going into the apartment ahead of her which caused her to react vehemently.

"Protecting 'the little woman,'" she said sarcastically.

" Hardly." Rick answered with a smile. "But I'm armed and you aren't I see. It's just a precaution," he continued. "Just like you, I was trained never to take unnecessary chances." He relaxed, stretching his long frame onto the small black leather couch and perching his running shoes gingerly on the edge of Janine's coffee table, covered with papers and notebooks.

"Well, you can start by getting your feet off my desk," she said, pouring him a drink, and settling down beside him with her soda water.

"So what's the problem?"

" How do you get a Saudi Princess, dead or alive, out of Paris, completely unnoticed?"

" Private plane, tipping everyone generously as you go."

"Even the French air control?"

"Hard to do. If there are a few incorruptible people left in the world, they probably work for French air control."

"Can you think of another way?"

"Large plastic body bag in the back of a limo," he said soberly. " But it's a long drive to the ocean and to a sea going vessel. Then you would have to get the body off the boat at the other end. Not necessarily a job without problems of its own," he finished, lifting his glass for a refill, and grinning.

Janine thought that he was getting entirely too sure of himself. She was almost sorry that she had asked him up. It was a moment of temporary weakness, she assured herself, as Rick's hand slowly massaged the back of her neck. It felt good, and familiar. She eased back into his arm, relaxing just a little. The warmth of his hand was comforting. She stifled a sigh.

"Did you really ask me up to talk about a missing Princess?"

"What else."

"I thought that you might be planning to seduce me," Rick grinned, resting his glass on the edge of the table and putting his arm around her.

His glass fell and shattered, spilling the contents on Janine's African rug and spoiling the moment. She leapt up grabbing a cloth from her tiny kitchen, and mopped furiously at the hand woven rug, muttering angrily as she scrubbed at the stain.

Rick shook his head. " You are a hard lady to seduce, even if I was trying," he smiled, standing up and heading for the door. "Just don't wander around unarmed anymore. I have the feeling that someone is too interested in what you are doing for your own good. If I were you, I would watch my back," he said pulling her to him in the doorway and kissing her firmly on her half open mouth.

Then he gave her a mock salute as he closed the door behind him. Leaving her standing for once, speechless.

Janine sat down again on the couch. Why did the evening feel like such an anti-climax? She knew Rick so well. Why did she feel that she was missing out on something really good in her life. They continually passed each other like two trains on different schedules. Sometimes it left her feeling really sad. Like tonight for example. They had a familiar but toxic attraction. They had given in to it in Tunisia with wrenching results when they parted to go their own ways. He still pulled at her. Making her remember their good times and forget the difficult ones. His ex-wife Melanie was still very much in the picture as was his college age son. She couldn't wean him from them five years ago. Why was she even thinking of trying again now?

Rick was a loner, just as she was, neither of them willing to compromise enough to have a real relationship. She wasn't even sure if she really wanted one. Love hurt too much. She had seen that when her Army father left her mother after getting her pregnant and bringing her to a foreign country where she barely spoke the language. She and her mother had survived, barely, but it had given Janine the streak of unbendable independence that she fostered so carefully.

Better to steer clear of beginning something with Rick again that she had no intention of finishing.

But his hands had felt so warm and familiar on her back, and his kiss had been soft and caring. Perhaps there was something to resurrect in their relationship after all. She would have to think about that. In the meantime she had a Saudi Princess to track down, dead or alive, and she needed to start fresh again in the morning.

Chapter Twenty Two

Jogging home in the soft light of street lamps reflecting off the Seine, Rick was mentally kicking himself. Why had he kissed her? He had no intention of getting involved with her again. She could turn on her heel and walk out at any moment, as she had done after Tunisia. She was a loner and didn't need anyone. It has just seemed tonight as though she was suddenly vulnerable. And that had attracted him, though he couldn't imagine why. There were plenty of other women in Paris who would enjoy spending time with him. And if they ended up in bed, well then so be it. Why Janine of all people? What was it about her that continually challenged and attracted him? He stopped suddenly and almost stumbled over the body of a man lying on the sidewalk. The smell of alcohol on the tramp was overwhelming. His clothes were soiled, and he looked as though he had been beaten and robbed of what little he had.

Rick helped the man up and then watched him lean against the wall. He was in no shape to walk anywhere. Rick had a sudden image of himself in that position, if he ever gave in to the demons that haunted him. The smell of alcohol on the man both repelled and attracted him at the same time. He shoved a ten franc note into the man's pocket and told him to get something to eat, and coffee to drink. The drunk looked at him with bleary eyes, his breath was terrible. But he seemed to realize that Rick was a friend. *"Merci, mon frère,"* he muttered incoherently, *"vous et un ange, merci a Dieu."* Rick wasn't sure that there was anything angelic about him or his deed. But it had taken his mind off Janine for the moment. And that was a blessing.

He continued jogging along the Seine. Looking up at the towers of Notre Dame, still illuminated at this hour of the evening. He loved this city. It was true what they said about Paris. She was a lover and a woman, probably the safest woman that he had ever loved and the most faithful. Certainly Janine wasn't faithful. She had been bad news from the beginning. Still she had promised nothing. Neither of them had. So whose fault had it really been that they had lost contact over the years? It was his as well as hers. She certainly had a difficult case to crack at the moment. There was no telling where the Saudi Princess had ended up. Unless she really was in a body bag somewhere, in the trunk of one of the royal limousines, until her brother could figure out how to get rid of her body permanently. No one back home in the palace would ask any questions. If it was a matter of Saudi honor, it was his job to solve it as he saw fit.

Shaking his head at his morbid thoughts, he jogged down a silent side street toward his lonely apartment. It would have been nice to have had someone sexy and warm, eager to welcome him home. He smiled, trying to imagine Janine in that role. She would more than likely be holding a gun on him, ready to shoot if he came near. No, that was not the image that taunted him tonight. It was of a younger Janine, lips parted, and eyes longing for him that he remembered faintly from Tunis, like the melody of a half-forgotten song. What he would give to see her like that again. Then he shook his head bitterly. That was not likely to ever happen again in this life. If she wanted him around, it was only to help her solve her case. This was only business, and nothing else, regrettably.

****

Janine had a difficult time going to sleep. She drank a cup of hot milk, laced with honey, smiling as she did so. It was her mother's remedy for a sleepless night, and she must have had many. It couldn't have been easy raising a daughter by herself in Paris. Perhaps that was why she had communicated so clearly to Janine her innate distrust of men. She had taught Janine to put her work and her own survival before relationships, as she herself had learned, so painfully, to do.

The detachment had stood Janine in good stead throughout most of her career. Kept her out of entanglements that might have slowed her down. Kept her from caring for anyone so much that it would have jeopardized her career, or her ability to move fast and reverse direction on a dime if needed. But now that skill was beginning to feel like a burden she wanted to put down. Just as she had begun to put down roots here on Rue Belle Chasse. Perhaps a relationship was possible with Rick after all these years. Was it worth a chance? Or was she just setting herself up for a final heartbreak?

The phone jangled harshly. Janine hesitated before answering it. Then deciding that it might be Rick, or possibly the office, she picked up the receiver. At first there was no answer to her response. Then as she was just about to hang up, a breathy woman's voice, speaking in Arabic began to beg for her help. She said that she was a prisoner, being held in a dark place. Someone had given her this number to call. Could Janine help her, she was so afraid. Then the phone line went dead. Janine tried to call the number back but it rang and rang and there was no answer. This was unnerving, particularly now when she was searching for the Princess. But no-one outside of her office had this number. She racked her brains to think of anyone that she might have given it to who was involved with the case. She suddenly remembered Madame Zebur's boutique. Had she given her number to Sari, her daughter, during their conversation? It was a possibility that she needed to follow up first thing in the morning.

****

She waited impatiently next morning for it to be late enough to visit Madame Zebur's boutique. She called several times to find what time they opened, but there was no answer. So she busied herself as long as she could, dealing with mail and paper work that she'd been avoiding for weeks. She had to submit a full report to the office on her visit to Algiers and she had been avoiding it since her return. She hated the paper work part of her job, which seemed to be getting more copious each year. Or maybe she was just getting older and less patient with it. She banged out a report on her newly refurbished laptop, and hoped that it would at least be in depth enough to keep the 'boys' off her back. After all, she had managed to protect the Minister. That was at least something in her favor, and certainly worth the trip.

Around ten o'clock she rang the boutique again, and getting no answer, she decided to go over and get a look for herself. It was a long shot, but she couldn't think of anything else to do after last night's strange phone call. Unless the call had been a hoax, the woman who had called her has certainly in trouble and afraid. But she hadn't a clue as to where to look for her or how to help her. Janine put on a red turtle neck sweater and scarf, black jeans and boots, and her long black leather coat and took a taxi to an address just off the Champs Elysees where she had had last seen Madame Zebur and her daughter.

The black lacquered door was closed and locked tight. Janine consulted her watch. It wasn't yet eleven o'clock. Perhaps she was too early. She strode around to the back of the building, and found herself in a cul-de-sac filled with trash bins and locked and bolted rear doors to the various shops. She walked to the end of the alley, looking for a clue as to where the Zeburs might have gone. A gray haired woman dressed the blue overalls worn by cleaning people, came out of the back door of one of the shops and stared at her intently, hands on hips, "What are you doing here, Madame?" she asked insolently. "You look too fine to be picking through our trash."

Janine hid a grin. It was the first time that she had even been mistaken for a rag and bone lady. "I am trying to find some evidence of the whereabouts of Madame Zebur and her daughter. I am a client," she continued smoothly, "and they have failed in a delivery to me of a very special order, for my wedding," she added as an afterthought, surprising herself.

"They are not usually found in the back alley," the woman muttered, dumping her trash with a clang in the large commercial trash bin behind the store she was cleaning. She continued to look at Janine suspiciously. "Their shop hasn't been open in several days," she added. "Perhaps they are gone to the south on vacation. That is what rich people do, I'm told." she sneered, closing the back door of the shop behind her with a bang.

Janine stayed by the Zebur's back door for a few moments, thinking. This would be a terrible time to try to break in. Besides the door was certainly alarmed. Unless Zebur had taken the jewelry with her, she had left behind a fortune in diamonds and rubies belonging to Princess Saroya. Surely the door would be locked. She gave it a gentle shove. It opened soundlessly. She glanced around, and seeing no one, she eased inside the darkened store. She was in a utility room filled with mops and an ancient refrigerator that gave off an insistent hum in the dark room, lightened only by a dusty skylight. Janine cautiously pushed open the door to the main boutique. It too was in half darkness, lightened only by skylights. Half clothed women stood around the room in various frightened poses. One was lying on the floor in a pool of blood with her head beside her.

Janine lurched back into the closet and then cautiously opened the door again to peer into the showroom. Her pocket flashlight revealed that what she was seeing were mannequins, wearing torn evening dresses and positioned to look terrified, their white plastic arms hiding their faces, their hands smeared with a red blood- like substance. The show room was trashed. Ripped evening dresses and *abaayas* were strewn about the floor and covered the runway. Rude sayings in Arabic were scratched into the walls in red paint or lipstick. The ones that Janine could translate didn't bode well for Madame Zebur or her daughter's future. There was no evidence of real blood or a struggle, except for the fortune in torn sample clothing that littered the floor, and the headless mannequins.

Near the blocked front door, Janine noticed a large black ledger lying half hidden under an overturned table. It was the book that she had signed when she had come uninvited to Madame Zebur's showing of her collection. Several pages were torn out of it, along with the page with her signature and telephone number. She hastily tore out the rest of the pages, then wiped off the cover of the book and threw it back under the table. There were certainly enough fingerprints on it so that hers wouldn't stand out. She quickly searched the dressing rooms and finding nothing but chaos, slipped out the back door into the alley way and around to the front of the building.

She debated calling the police and then thought better of it. It might be difficult to explain how she had gained entrance. Perhaps one of Madame Zebur's clients would become suspicious when they couldn't retrieve their merchandise and call the local gendarmerie. It was better for her to stay out of it for the moment. She walked down the Champs Elysees, until she found a crowded tourist bistro doing a lively business at this hour of the morning. She ordered a double espresso and sat at the back of the room at a small table and examined the sheets that she had torn out of the ledger. Most of the handwriting was difficult to decipher, and the addresses, when there were any, were even more difficult.

Most of the addresses that she could read, were from very expensive hotels, understandable given wealth of the women that she had observed at the showing. She saw Saroya's name on one of the crumpled pages and an address at the Ritz hotel. But there was also another address in smaller writing, as though added as an afterthought. And this was the clue that Janine focused on. If the Princess had another address in Paris, could that be where they might be holding her? Janine took a deep breath and slowly finished her bitter coffee. If this was a clue to the Princess's whereabouts, she'd better not tackle it alone.

Chapter Twenty Three

Her curiosity being what it was, she decided to just swing by the address and see what kind of building it was in. The address was in the 7th arrondisement on Rue Fauberg, which was behind Les Invalides and almost next to the Air France terminal where busses left on the hour for Orly airport. It was a good neighborhood but not exactly a swanky one. Not the sort of place that Janine would have thought that the Princess would keep a secret apartment.

The building was an older elegant home, which had been renovated recently into apartments. There were signs that the work was still going on. Ladders were poised on the outside of the building and workmen in white overalls were repairing the crumbling plaster on the outside walls. The entry doors weren't locked. Possibly to accommodate the plasterers who looked Janine over casually as she strode inside, trying to look as though she was on a legitimate errand.

Just inside the door there was a rack of mailboxes, some with names, and some with business cards pushed into the slots for names. The apartment number that Saroya had written down had a man's name on a crumpled business card casually shoved into the too small slot. The name was in Arabic script and in English and the last name looked like Hassan. The first name was unreadable. The box was bulging with mail and there was even some on the floor addressed to the same apartment. Looking around carefully, Janine picked up a flyer addressed to Col Safi Hassan (ret), and hastily stuck it in her pocket. At least she now had the full name of the owner of the apartment and the fact that he hadn't picked up his mail in several days.

She saw a concierge sign over one of the doors on the first landing and decided to take a chance with a few questions. The workmen were now watching her carefully. She gave them a reassuring smile and walked up the stairs to the first landing. The doors were heavy oak and had recently been refurbished. The hallway smelled of turpentine and furniture oil. Not at all an unpleasant odor. She pressed the buzzer on the door, it sounded as loud as a fire alarm, presumably to wake the Concierge during the night if needed. A sour faced woman answered the door on the third ring.

She looked Janine over carefully, before saying in heavily accented French that there was nothing to rent in the building. "*Nous sommes complet*", she hissed, attempting to slam the door in Janine's face. But Janine was too fast for her; she stuck the toe of her solid black boot in the doorway, forcing the woman to keep it open an inch or two. "I have a message for Colonel Hassan" she said in her most authoritative voice. "Can you tell me when he will be returning?"

At the mention of Hassan's name, the old woman relented a little. Opening the door a crack wider and looking Janine up and down again, carefully. "Who is the message from?" she grumbled. "The Colonel is on vacation."

"I see that his mail has not been picked up," Janine said, in what she hoped was a neutral voice.

The woman took umbrage any way. "I do not have a key to his box. The second one was lost," she snarled. "What business is it of yours?"

"Only that his employers are trying to get in touch with him, and since his phone is not being answered, they have written to him with new instructions," Janine improvised.

The old woman looked puzzled, "But he no longer works for the company. He turned in his resignation weeks ago." Then she looked stricken as though she had inadvertently given away privileged information, which indeed she had.

Playing her winning hand, Janine continued. "But they still wish to contact him; did he perhaps leave a forwarding address?"

The old woman looked at her slyly, "I think that he wishes not to make contact with the Saudi's, that is why he went away on vacation." She smiled showing several broken teeth. "There are some things that a man will not do, even for money," and then for emphasis, she slammed the door shut firmly in Janine's face.

Janine smiled. She was a great deal closer to unraveling the puzzle of Saroya's disappearance. There was a man involved. And he too had been missing from Paris for about the same length of time as the Princess. He was using the title of a retired Colonel, but from which service? With a name like Hassan, it could be any one of the Arab states, or he could even be a French citizen.

She decided to involve Sam again. He still had excellent contacts in military intelligence. He was delighted to get her call, but somewhat evasive about his chances of locating a retired officer from another service. But after a few moments of teasing banter, he said that he would try. Janine gave him her cell phone number, and asked him to get back to her as soon as possible. She hoped that she had a really good lead, at last.

To kill some time while she waited for his phone call, she walked across the street to the entrance of the Hotel Des Invalides and Napoleon's tomb. In all the years that she had lived in Paris, she had never visited it. She didn't notice the tall, thin Arab wearing a long black coat, who watched her from the shadows of the apartment building. As she descended the steps and entered the gray marble mausoleum, she understood why. Napoleon was surrounded with all the glory of a fallen saint. Giant statues of morning gods surrounded his huge maroon sarcophagus poised on a raised dais in the middle of a sunken floor.

There was total silence as the arena was completely deserted. It didn't seem to be on a lot of tourist's lists. Janine understood why, the atmosphere was gloomy in the extreme, and there was no place to sit down. One had to stand a look at the sarcophagus with reverence or something approaching it, Janine supposed. She walked around the room studying it from all angles. Above her on the first level balcony the young man in a long black coat watched her with malicious attention, then began to move down toward her.

Just then her cell phone jangled, the sound reverberating on the marble walls. It would have been loud enough to wake the dead, if the dead were listening. She hurried up the stairs, for better reception as she answered, and to get out of the frigid atmosphere of the tomb. Sam's voice on the other end of the line was jubilant. "I found him for you," he chortled, "and on the second try. He isn't French. He is retired from the Jordanian Royal Air Force with honors. He may be some distant relative of the King." Sam paused dramatically, "But this is the kicker, since his retirement he had been piloting for the Saudi royal family on their private jets, and he may still be working for an organization similar to yours."

"Sam you are an angel and I owe you a lunch," Janine said jubilantly. "This is the first decent lead that I've had on this case."

"How about dinner?" Sam crooned into the phone.

"We might just do that," Janine answered. " But right now I'm tied up with Napoleon."

The man who watched her from the shadows had been listening avidly to her side of the conversation. He had almost had her alone in the tomb. If her telephone hadn't rung when it did, she would have joined the Emperor by now. Her scarlet blood would have stained the gray marble of the degenerate Emperor of France. The assassin would have enjoyed watching her die and begging for his mercy. He hid his knife in his long black coat, and strolled casually away from the monument. Looking like an ordinary student out for a walk.

Janine shuddered. She had felt as though someone was watching her in the tomb, but there had been no one around that she had seen. She pulled her red scarf more tightly around her neck. A cold breeze had begun to blow and the leaves, red orange and saffron, were whirling across the lawn. Now she had a name and a profession for the person who lived at the address that Saroya had hastily scribbled in Madame Z's notebook. Now she had to figure out what to do with the information. It had gotten her no closer to Saroya dead or alive.

She hurried home to do a computer search on the name Safi Hassan. She was almost too lucky. Her computer complied by tossing out hundreds of men with that name. When she narrowed the search by adding the title Colonel she got a few less hits, but it was still quite a list to go through. It took her most of the afternoon. By the time that she had narrowed the list even further, she thought that she might have a hit. But it was a strange one. The name Hassan kept coming up associated with a distribution of essential perfume oils in Grasse in the South of France. Checking Google maps, she found the town in the hills above Monaco. It looked like an untouched part of the coast; rolling hills covered with lavender, roses and all the other plants used for perfume making. It was a strange association for a Colonel from the Jordanian army, if it was indeed his family's property.

She located a few small bed and breakfasts, and an inn or two, listed in and around Grasse, on the internet. Janine decided to book one on the outskirts of the village for two nights. This would give her time to poke around over the weekend and see what she could turn up about the Hassan family. It looked as though they were fairly large landowners for that part of France, and had been there for some time. What better place to hide the Saudi Princess, if Col Hassan had taken her home with him. It was a long shot, but Janine felt in her gut that it was one worth taking, assuming that the Princess wasn't dead or abducted by her brother. There might be a chance that she was with her family's former pilot who just happened to be part of the Jordanian royal family and a fellow spook to boot.

It was worth a chance, and Janine was never one to ignore a chance when it presented itself.

Chapter Twenty Four

She called Sam, and told his answering machine that she was following up on the lead that he had given her, and would be out of town for a few days in the South near Monaco. She grinned. That should be enough to peak his curiosity, but not satisfy it completely. She promised to give him the details at lunch when she returned after the weekend.

Throwing a pair of slacks, a sweater, a bathing suit and some good hiking shoes into a carry all, along with her Beretta, she caught a taxi to the Gare De Lyon and bought a roundtrip ticket to Cannes. She could rent a car there and have some flexibility when she got to Grasse. There was a fast train in the late afternoon, so she decided to wait in the station to board it and save time rather than bumping along on the earlier slower train. She was eating a bagette aux jambon and drinking espresso in the station bar, when she felt a light touch on her shoulder. She whirled around, ready to respond to attack and found Rick and Sam grinning at her.

"We thought that you might need reinforcements," Rick said charmingly. "Besides I love Monaco. I'm quite a gambler you know."

"No, I didn't know, and I don't need help." Janine said, trying to glare at both of them at the same time. "If we go tramping around like combat troops, we will totally blow my cover."

"Well, it may already be blown," Sam said diffidently. "I have seen several people hanging around your apartment that are on the unsavory side."

Janine shook her head impatiently. "Some kid is trying to make a name for himself, by following me."

"Well, that kid has a vicious knife and an even worse reputation." Sam said firmly.

"Take it or leave it, one of us is going ride down to your destination with you this afternoon."

"Are you going to decide by flipping a coin," Janine asked caustically. "Or do I get to decide who my 'protector' is going to be?"

"Why don't we just let somebody kill her?" Rick snarled, shaking his head in disgust.

" Because I'm really very fond of her," Sam answered, attempting to put his arm around Janine.

She shook it off and glared at them. "I have a gun in my bag and could shoot you both right now. Would that settle the argument?"

"Probably, but that wouldn't get you to the south of France," Sam chuckled.

"Let Rick go along as your devoted fiancé or husband or sidekick, whichever you prefer. This is not a good time to go it alone, Janine," he said seriously. "You have definitely gotten some very unsavory people on your tail."

"And this Hassan character may not like you snooping around his family estate. If it is the same guy." Rick added. "Anyhow, I volunteer to ride down with you and help check out the situation. If we don't find anything, we can just call it a failed honeymoon."

Janine shook her head and paid for her coffee and sandwich, thinking over the situation.

It was more trouble to get rid of them in the station than it was worth. She decided that she could lose Rick when they changed trains in Marseilles. It would be dark, and she had a car waiting for her at the station in Cannes. It would be easy to get rid of Rick even there, if she decided that he was getting in her way. In the meantime he might be company on the five-hour train ride.

She smiled at him with a glint in her eye. "I suppose that you know what you are doing," she said caustically. "This has nothing to do with your project in Algeria."

"Well, we don't know that for sure," he replied. " Most things in the Arab world that concern terrorists are connected somehow, haven't you learned that by now ?"

Janine had to agree, despite herself. What he said was true. There were too many loose ends and too many coincidences in this affair to make her comfortable. She was going to Grasse mostly because she didn't have another lead at the moment. Having Rick along might not be a bad idea. But she sure wasn't going to let him know it.

Sam left, mentally tipping his hat at the both of them and grinning to himself. He hadn't gotten over a romantic streak even at his age. And somehow he felt that Rick and Janine were made for each other. They both were smart, stubborn and too independent for their own good. A trip to the south of France together might be just what they needed to put aside their grudges and have some fun together. That is, if they didn't kill each other in the process.

Janine, on the other hand, had decided to ignore Rick once they boarded the train. This wasn't difficult since they shared their carriage with a young mother with two small male children, who did their best to imitate all the sound the train was making, and then some. The woman looked at the couple apologetically, but did nothing to stifle her boys' energy. Finally, to Janine's amazement, Rick took over, launching into a number of train imitations that had the little boys rocking with laughter. It was loud but not hysterical noise and the young mother looked at Rick with something more than gratitude in her eyes.

Janine buried her head in a magazine and pretended not to watch. It was the first time that she had seen Rick with children, and it wasn't difficult to imagine him with his own son, Robbie, years ago when the boy was young. From what she had heard from Sam she knew that the two were somehow estranged. Which was a shame, after all Rick had gone through to rescue him from dissidents in Tunisia, five years ago.

She put those thoughts firmly out of her mind. That was then and this was now. Their mutual attraction had come out of need and the excitement of pursuing a mutual enemy. It had come to nothing because of both of their separate careers. And it would come to nothing now. This was just Sam's fantasy that they were playing out. But she acknowledged that Rick was a good man in a show-down, if it came to that. So she smiled over at him encouragingly, much to his surprise.

The train clattered along though the late afternoon's fragile sunlight. The motions lulled the two little boys to sleep and the compartment got silent and increasingly stuffy. Janine glanced at Rick. He was deep in a book, seemingly paying no attention. She got up and stretched and headed out the door to the toilet, checking her cell phone for messages as she went along the corridor. Someone had called several times without leaving a message. It was an unfamiliar number, and when she tried to return the call a recorded voice asked her to leave a message. She said that she was out of town and could probably be reached later at this same number. Puzzled she kept walking through the train to the buffet car in search of coffee.

The cold air as she maneuvered between cars was refreshing. She began to plan what she would do when she got to Grasse. Having Rick along was a bit of a complication, unless they followed Sam's suggestion and posed as a vacationing couple. That scenario had its benefits as a cover story. But she wasn't too sure that she wanted Rick's company for three days. Things might get complicated, and she didn't need or want any complications in her life at the moment.

Her cell phone rang again. She answered it cautiously, but the voice on the other end was anything but cautious. It was Rick and he was furious. "Where the hell are you!" he fumed. "If I am supposed to be helping you in this hair brained scheme of yours, don't wander off without telling me. I'm not sure that this train is secure. And it would be a good idea to arrive in Grasse with both of us alive."

"Not to worry," Janine said soothingly. "I've just gone to get coffee."

"You drink too much of that stuff. You are going to rot your stomach."

"I'm trying to stay awake until we reach Marseilles where we change trains. You were deep in your book."

"Just stay in the club car till I get there. And don't talk to strangers."

Janine cut off the connection abruptly. Who did he think he was? Her self appointed watch dog.

But when he arrived in the club car he was grinning charmingly. He seated himself across from her at a table and patted her hand.

Despite herself, Janine smiled. It was good to have backup. She had the feeling that they were riding into the unraveling of this convoluted case and it might be good to have Rick along.

Chapter Twenty Five

They changed trains in Marseilles with only a few moments to spare. It was a very tight connection and the train to Cannes was on a far track. They arrived just in time, dragging their carry alls behind them. The station was filled with passengers of all descriptions. Quite a few Arab guest workers climbed aboard behind them, talking and joking in Arabic and bringing with the sounds and odors of bazaars of the world. Janine wrinkled her nose; she would recognize that sound and smell anywhere.

"There must be jobs in Grasse, in the essential oils factories or picking flowers," Rick said scanning the workers carefully. "It would be relatively easy for a terrorist to hide with this crowd and never be noticed."

Janine nodded, they were in unfamiliar territory and it would be good to be extra cautious. The found seats in the first class carriage and left the guest workers behind, temporarily. But when they got to Cannes, they all exploded off the train together. Janine headed for the car agency and was relieved that they had saved a late model Citroen for her. The drive to Grasse was only about twenty miles and the road was straight along the coast most of the way. As they started up into the hills the road got less well traveled. It circled back on itself, and made narrow turns as they climbed up into the hills behind the coast. They could see the lights of Monaco in the distance, shimmering like lost stars. Janine was driving and had to keep her eyes on the road. But she wasn't immune to the beauty and the haunting perfume of flowers in the air.

When they arrived at the small inn where Janine had reserved a room, she stopped the car to admire the view over the hills to the ocean. She could see the lights of cruise ships far away in the bay. But up in the hills it was dark and filled with the tantalizing scents of lavender and roses. She wondered how she was going to explain Rick's presence, but decided that the best strategy was to lie through her teeth as usual. The innkeeper didn't seem concerned with renting an additional room, despite Rick's protestations that he and Janine could share if necessary. Janine rolled her eyes at his suggestion and the Inn keeper seemed amused at *Les Americans*.

Not to waste any time, Janine inquired about the Hassan Essential Oil factory, and if they had visiting hours.. The innkeeper beamed and told her that indeed they were very fortunate, since some of the late blooms were now being harvested. So the factory was open to the public at two o'clock every afternoon for tours and an explanation about how the oil for some of France's most famous perfume houses were extracted. He also gave them a brochure of some of the other interesting walks around the city, including the famous caverns in the hills behind the town.

Janine thanked him and handed him her credit card, but Rick insisted in using his instead for their adjoining rooms. This was to the obvious amusement of the innkeeper who was rapidly gathering some interesting stories to tell his cronies about *les amants American.*

Janine decided not to argue. She had enough to worry about without hassling Rick in public about who paid the bill. If it made him feel manly and in control that was just fine with her, for the moment.

Her highest priority now, was how to get into the Hassan complex without waiting for the public tour the next afternoon. Patience had never been her long suit, and it certainly wasn't now. Not with the life of the Saudi Princess possibly part of the equation.

Rick inquired where they could still get supper in town. The innkeeper grimaced sadly. Most of the restaurants were closing early, since it was off season. But he could offer them soup and bread in his breakfast room if that would suffice for the night. Glancing at Janine, Rick accepted for them promptly. Janine glared at him, she would have preferred to walk into the village and get the lay of the land. Patting her hand fondly, Rick explained that his fiancée was *fatigue'* and would love some good *'soupe du Provence'* before retiring for the night.

Janine was now gritting her teeth and regretting allowing Rick to get this far with the pretense of being engaged. A stupid term at their ages anyhow. But he seemed to have charmed the portly innkeeper, who after showing them their adjoining rooms, invited them into a spotless small dining room with round tables looking out into a darkened garden. The scent of lavender permeated the room. There were sprigs of it and other provincial herbs on each table, brightly decorated with yellow and red tablecloths.

Janine sank into one of the cushioned, bent-work chairs, and realized suddenly how tired she was. The memory of her bedroom waiting upstairs with its huge canopied bed, danced before her eyes, which she struggled to keep open. The soup was hot, spicy and completely satisfying and the warm bread that accompanied it seemed sent from heaven. The thought of wandering the darkened streets of the village seemed farther and farther away as she struggled not to fall asleep with her head in the soup.

She followed Rick upstairs, yawning and ignoring his amused expression, closed and locked her door, falling into bed without even washing her face. She wondered briefly if Rick had drugged her soup. She felt such an unusual sense of utter relaxation. If this was what the air of Provence did to the body, then they should name it, bottle it and sell it as a cure for insomnia.

Chapter Twenty Six

Janine woke once in the night to the sound of rustling outside her window. She struggled up and looked outside. It was only the branch of a tree blowing gently back and forth across the open window, which she had neglected to secure. The smell of lavender and other aromatic herbs was almost overwhelming. She struggled into her pajamas and brushed her teeth. She couldn't remember how long it had been since she had slept like this, out of time, forgetting everything. She stumbled back into bed after closing the window, reluctantly. The soothing aroma of lavender still filled the room and lulled her back to sleep.

When Rick knocked on her door in the morning, she was already up and dressed and ready for coffee. They ate breakfast at the same small table, now festooned with wildflowers. The coffee was hot and strong and the breakfast rolls tasted as though they had just come out of a bakers oven. It would be easy to forget why they had come here and just revel in the hospitality of the innkeeper, who seemed to regard them with a proprietary air. He was a bit too curious about their plans for the day, and Janine found herself extracting herself from his questions by waving one of the brightly printed brochures from the lobby at him.

"We really haven't decided yet," she said firmly, "but you can be sure that we plan to take in as many of the local attractions as possible while we are here. I am especially interested in the manufacture of the essential oils for perfume, that have gone on here for hundreds of years. I understand that the process hasn't changed much in all that time."

The innkeeper beamed at her knowledge, gathered just recently from the brochure she waved in his direction, as she and Rick escaped through the front door.

The day was cool but sunny and the village was already alive with shoppers and tourists. Janine wondered if this was off-season what full season must be like. They wandered through the village, getting the lay of the land. The Hassan complex was further up the hill and by mutual agreement she and Rick decided not to wait for two o'clock for the general tour but see if they could barge in early.

"Maybe your business card for the chemical company could get us an early tour." Janine suggested. "Anyhow, its worth a try."

"Except that we don't produce the kind of chemicals that they use in perfume. And chemical use is frowned upon by the essential oil manufacturers, I understand."

"That's even better," Janine answered. "A little controversy can cover up the real reason for our visit."

"And that would be?" Rick grinned.

"To get a line on Colonel Safi Hassan. To see if he and the Princess are in residence."

" And how are we going to do that?"

"I haven't the slightest idea."

****

The Hassan factory was at the top of the hill behind the village. It was surrounded by what seemed like acres of white and pink roses and tall clumps of lavender waving gently in the morning breeze. The aroma was wonderful and the air was filled with the sound of bees and humming birds going about their work of collecting nectar.

The building itself was much smaller than Janine had imagined. Though she really had no idea what an essential oil factory would look like. The main building was of aged rose colored brick, covered with flowering vines. The massive front door was open and the smaller buildings on each side of the main house were also open for workers carrying in baskets of aromatic blooms. The workmen nodded at Janine and Rick as they passed, but continued with their tasks. However, they must have alerted someone inside the main building, because, in a few minutes, a dark haired young woman in a flowered smock, came out of the main house and approached the visitors.

" May I help you?" she asked in curiously accented French. Janine replied in French that they were interested in seeing how the essential oils were extracted from the flowers.

The young woman looked regretful and replied that they were not doing that work today, only gathering the flowers in preparation.' Perhaps if they came back later they could take the public tour of the facility at two o'clock.'

Janine glanced at Rick, who put on his most charming smile. Holding out his card he explained that he represented a chemical company who was interested in how the oils were constituted.

The young woman looked at his card, thoroughly flustered, as though he had offered her a snake. "We do not use chemicals, Monsieur," she replied firmly, in English. "We only preserve the pure essence of flowers as we have done for hundreds of years. Perhaps you were misinformed."

Rick pretended to be offended at the news. "Perhaps I could speak to the owner of the factory," he said firmly. "I was informed that he might be interested in purchasing some of our products."

The young woman looked even more upset. "My father would never do such a thing," she insisted, her voice getting louder in protest. " Pure Hassan oils have been used in perfumes throughout the Middle East and in Europe for generations."

A short gray haired man wearing a blue smock and worn trousers of the same material, came out of the front door and walked in their direction, His eyes were dark brown and his skin the color of old leather. He put his hand firmly on the young woman's shoulder, either to comfort her or to make her stop talking, Janine couldn't tell which.

"I am Hatim Hassan, the owner of this establishment, may I help you?" he asked looking the visitors over very carefully. "It sounds as though there may have been a misunderstanding .We do not add chemicals to our product. They are totally pure flower essence."

"Then I was misinformed," Rick answered graciously. "My fiancée and I are here on a vacation, and thought that we would take the opportunity to see how your oils are produced. The chemical inquiry was only an afterthought, since I am in that business. But we did not mean to offend your daughter in any way," he finished warmly.

Hassan looked somewhat appeased, though still suspicious. He glanced at Janine, who seething inwardly at being dismissed as Rick's fiancée, put on her best professional smile. "Is it possible that while we are here we could just look around a bit and perhaps take a few pictures? It is such a fascinating and traditional craft from this part of France."

Her engaging manner must have won the elderly man over somewhat. He nodded graciously, ignoring the warning glance his daughter gave him. "My daughter Fatima can give you a short tour, if you wish, this morning. But if you want a fuller explanation of all we do, you really should come back this afternoon." Then with a firm glance at his daughter, he disappeared back into the main building which seemed to serve as both home and factory office.

Fatima seemed confused by her father's request. She glanced at the clipboard in her hand, and then shrugged, shaking her head in annoyance. "If you can wait here for a few moments, I will finish giving the workmen instructions and then come back to take you on a very short tour," she said in polite exasperation. Then she turned on her heel, and quickly followed her father into the house.

"Checking with dad as to what she should show us," Janine said under her breath as she sat down on the edge of a small fountain. "I have the feeling that this won't take long."

"Maybe just long enough to find out if Safi is related to this family, and if by any chance he is visiting," Rick said, glancing around curiously. The workmen had disappeared and the courtyard was now quiet. It was as though their arrival had disturbed the normal activity of the morning, and the whole place was holding its breath, waiting for them to leave.

The young woman returned in a few moments. She had removed her smock and pinned back her hair with a gold clip, making her appear even younger. She had clearly been given her marching orders by her father, and she was determined to do her professional duty by them. She led them firmly away from the house and into the gardens beyond, which were fragrant with late blooms. As she explained the harvesting process, several workmen watched them curiously. This was certainly not the time for regular tours. The workers were all olive skinned and dark eyed. They glanced down when Janine smiled directly at them, a sure sign of Arab discomfort or courtesy.

Fatima's explanations went on and on. The sun was getting hotter and they were not getting any closer to finding out what they had come for. Was Safi a member of this family and was he by any chance here? Janine began to fan herself and to move back toward the main house, much to Fatima's discomfort. "There is more to see here," she insisted, "I have not finished my explanations."

" You are very kind and know a great deal that is very interesting," Janine insisted politely. "But I really must trouble you for a drink of water. Is it possible to go into the main factory for a moment to get something to drink?"

The young woman looked troubled, her ingrained Arab courtesy toward a guest, struggling with the instructions that her father had given her about keeping them away from the house. But courtesy won out. "If you do not mind coming with me to my mother's kitchen, I'm sure that we can offer you a cooling drink," she said graciously, at the same time glancing nervously toward the main house.

"That would be delightful," Janine answered promptly. "I think that we have learned enough about your operation to assuage our interest. And we both thank you for all the excellent information that you have given us."

Fatima blushed at the compliment. Janine had the feeling that she didn't receive many in her position as tour guide and daughter. She led them slowly toward the back of the main house, talking on her cell phone to inform someone that they were coming. Rick looked over at Janine with raised eyebrows. Security was pretty tight here, if all they were doing her was producing scented oils for perfume.

Hatim Hassan met them outside the back door, holding out a glass of water for Janine. It was clear that not even Arab courtesy was going to get them inside the main house. He smiled in a friendly manner, ushering them toward their waiting car. After Janine had slowly finished the water, she handed him her glass, and glancing once more back toward the house, thanked him profusely for the tour. "Your daughter knows quite a bit about the processing of perfume oils," she said making polite conversation.

Hatim glanced proudly at his daughter. "She is the only child I have that is interested in our trade. It is too bad she is a girl. Our secrets will die with me."

"And so you have many secrets?" Janine asked ingeniously.

Hatim looked her over carefully. "Every industry has secrets," he said pulling open their car door. "Some are more carefully kept than others. Ours can only be passed to a male member of the family." He closed the car door firmly behind her, almost slamming it in his hurry to get them off the property.

"Well, that was amusing and unproductive." Rick said, as they drove off. "Do you have any more ideas about how to charm the Hassans out of their family secrets?"

"Well, we know that something more than perfume oil is making them nervous about having strangers on the property," Janine said confidently. "Now we just have to find out what that is."

"And just how are we going to go about that?" Rick challenged.

"I'm working on that. I'll tell you after lunch," she grinned. "I'm starving."

Chapter Twenty Seven

Lunch was a silent and hurried affair. Rick picked out a small bistro on the main street of the old town and ordered lunch while Janine gazed into the distance. She seemed totally immune to the charm of the setting this morning. All her considerable energy was focused on the problem at hand, how to get into the Hassan stronghold and have a look around. Short of breaking into the house in the middle of the night, she hadn't a clue how to do it. Rick was smiling at her annoyingly. "No master plan as yet" he chided her over his fragrant dish of fish, simmering in a light wine sauce.

" I know that they are hiding something," she sputtered.

"But has it ever occurred to you that they just don't want outside visitors in their home. It doesn't mean that they are hiding the Princess."

"But they could be. What if she came here with their son or brother, whoever Safi might be, and they are protecting both of them."

"Have you ever considered writing detective novels?" Rick joshed taking a sip of his Perrier water. " You might be really good at it."

Janine kicked him under the table. " Then help me think this plot through. How would you get in to have a look around?"

Rick thought for a minute. Then he grinned. "Why not go back this afternoon when they have the public tour. If it's a large group, they will be less on the alert for someone poking around. Besides I can always confess that the lovely Fatima entranced me so much that I had to see her again."

"And risk getting skinned alive by her Arab papa?" Janine answered. "I think that you had better leave the explanations to me. If they find us wandering around where we shouldn't be. I'll think of something."

They spent the next few hours exploring the lovely old village, asking subtle questions about the Hassan family, and getting nowhere. At the mention of the name the villagers gave them odd looks and changed the subject immediately. They were freely offered perfume for sale, knock offs of famous brands, bunches of flowers, even home made jams and jellies with a basis of flower petals, but no information about the Hassans.

"Ether they have nothing to hide or they are paying off the local merchants not to gossip about them. It's very frustrating." Janine said, after having purchased her third pot of rose petal jelly from a local merchant dressed in bright gingham and lace. "It's a little like being in OZ."

"Maybe there really isn't anything to gossip about," Rick said thoughtfully. "Has that possibility even occurred to you?"

"Yes, but I haven't given up on the other angle," Janine said firmly. "Not until we have taken another look."

That's why they found themselves standing in line with a large group of French tourists for the two p.m. tour of the perfume factory. They had changed clothes and were standing at the back of the line, hoping not to appear too conspicuous when Fatima saw them again. But she didn't give an overt sign of recognition. They decided to take advantage of her discretion and stay at the back of the line as she led the group up to the front door of the house and into a large area that served as a reception room and shop. There were vials of essential oils from a number of flowers, which she allowed the visitors to handle and to smell. Then she launched into an explanation of how each of the oils was made.

During this time, Janine was looking around for a way into the rest of the house. Rick shook his head at her firmly, but ignoring him, she slipped through a door at the back of the room that led into a hallway. This seemed to lead to the private quarters of the family. She could smell cooking and heard voices coming from the end of the hall. They were speaking in a mixture of French and Arabic and the voices were raised in some kind of controversy.

Sliding down the hall carefully, so as not to make any noise, she thought that she heard the name Safi several times. It was a man's voice obviously raised in anger. Women's voices countered his in protest, speaking Arabic. Could they really be standing up to the master of the house? That was odd in an Arab household, even one that has been living in France as long as this one had. Then she was sure that she heard the name Saroya, uttered defiantly by one of the women. She was about to edge closer when the door flew open and Hatim stormed into the hall. He reacted violently when he saw Janine. For a moment she thought that he was going to strike her.

She backed away, shrugging her shoulders and attempting to look helpless. Not easy when you are five foot ten in stocking feet. She looked around searchingly and asked for the "WC," then "toilette," and "ladies room," in what she hoped was an appealing tone.

Angry with her, but also embarrassed by this duty, which he considered way below his dignity, he led her back along the hallway and almost shoved her into a clearly marked door just outside the main showroom. Janine entered hurriedly, cursing her luck.

When she came out a few minutes later Hatim had disappeared, but Fatima was waiting for her, looking troubled. "My father was not pleased that you had left the group," she said glancing around hurriedly. "Please do me the favor to stay with me for the rest of the tour, or it will not be pleasant for you and your husband."

She led Janine back into the showroom where the other tourists were milling around, smelling the essential oils, in decorative vials, and purchasing many of them. Rick stood in the corner of the room surrounded by several older women who were chatting him up. He gestured helplessly to Janine who approached him grinning and taking his arm. "Hey, you could have linked up with a rich French widow while I was gone," she teased.

"Getting yourself strangled in the back halls of the house?"

"No, just persona non grata."

"You already had that distinction," he said, leading her back to the car. " I would be very surprised if Hatim and family let us near the place again. You seem to have broken all the rules of Arab courtesy, and some that don't even exist."

Janine climbed into the car with a look on her face like a cat who has just finished a bowl of cream. "But they know something about the Princess and Safi. I heard their names in an argument coming from the kitchen, before Hatim dragged me off to show me the lady's room. I know that we are on the right track now."

"And exactly what do you propose that we do about it? Call in the Marines?"

"No, let's call Sam and organize some back up, before we go in tonight."

"Lady you are out of your mind. Breaking and entering goes way beyond what you are authorized to do."

"Maybe that's why I'm enjoying it so much," she said, punching him playfully on the shoulder.

He grabbed her by the arms and pulled her to him, kissing her firmly, and for a long time.

She finally pulled away, looking surprised and a bit shocked. "What did you do that for?" she said, catching her breath.

"I wanted to see if it still worked," he answered, smiling. " That's one reason why I prefer that you give up on this project before you get yourself killed or maimed for life. I have begun to enjoy having you around again."

Janine shook her head, ignoring the ringing in her ears that his kiss had started. "Well, then you know me better than to think I will give up on a search just because some irate Arab wants me to. But believe me I will think it through before I go back in there single handed."

Chapter Twenty Eight

But she was lying. After a quiet dinner in one of the charming bistros that lined the main street of the village, and then lying to a surprised Rick saying she wanted to turn in early. She waited impatiently in her room until the village clock struck eleven. Then she slid down the stairs quietly and put the car in neutral, pushing it downhill to the corner of the street. Then she climbed in and drove up the hill again and parked a few blocks from the Hassan's factory. The street was silent. An occasional street lamp cast an eerie glow in the direction of the house. Glad that she had seen no dogs around on her earlier visit, she crept around the house to the kitchen door. It was surrounded by thick shrubbery that had recently been watered. She swore as she stepped into mud that was almost ankle deep, giving her a reason to take off her shoes and put them outside the door.

She listened for a few minutes. Then hearing nothing, she tried the door again. It was an ancient French lock that she quickly dismantled with her pocket knife. She paused again, listening for sounds of activity in the house. But everything was silent. Holding her breath, she pushed the door open silently, then hesitated as it creaked on its ancient hinges. Once inside, she hesitated again until her eyes grew accustomed to the darkness. She was in a kind of mud room outside the main kitchen. It was filled with rubber boots and shovels, the kind of thing that would be in any home that maintained a large commercial garden.

She heard a noise and froze in her tracks. It seemed to be coming from the kitchen. There was no light from under the door, so whoever was in there was also in darkness. She heard something hit the floor and break and a veiled exclamation of anger or frustration, she couldn't tell which. Then the door to the mud room opened slowly, and a figure appeared. Janine backed silently toward the rear door, scarcely breathing. The figure moved toward her in the darkness, holding something in an outstretched hand. She backed further toward the wall, holding her breath.

Her shoulder must have hit a light switch, because suddenly the room was illuminated. A frightened child, who looked about eight years old, was standing in front of her holding a piece of cake in an outstretched hand. "Are you the ghost?" the child said in a frightened voice, "If you are, here is some cake to eat if you won't hurt me. Please take it and let me go."

Janine nodded, speechless. She had been accused of many things in her life, but never of being a ghost, and never by a child. She nodded slowly and took the offered cake from the child's outstretched hand. " It is time you returned to bed," she said in French. "This is just a dream that you will not even remember me in the morning."

"But why have you come?" the child asked breathlessly. "Did you come to take the pretty lady away? She cries often in the night to go home."

" Where is she?" Janine asked warily. This was all getting too spooky to be true.

The child smiled cunningly. "Papa will take her away because she cries too loudly in the night. I don't cry because I don't want them to take me away too." She smiled enchantingly at Janine, who had a sudden urge to take the child in her arms and comfort her.

But this feeling was suddenly reversed by a harsh voice coming from the hallway. "What are you doing sneaking into the kitchen at night for food?" the voice demanded angrily in French. "Your papa will spank you if he finds you here."

The little girl turned toward the door as Janine snapped off the light, hoping that the darkness would cover her presence. But she was not so lucky. " I was talking to the ghost," the child said defensively. "Besides papa did not give me any desert because he said that I was naughty. But the ghost likes me."

Janine stood stock still in the dark mud-room. Hoping that whoever had come for the child would take her back to bed and not investigate further. She heard the kitchen door slam shut and then there was silence. She stood frozen in the darkness, scarcely breathing, as she backed toward the door.

Suddenly an arm was around her neck and another pinned her arms behind her. She was choking, struggling for air and for her gun when, the arm tightened around her throat and everything went black.

Chapter Twenty Nine

Rick woke from a troubling dream with a strong feeling that something wasn't right. At first he couldn't remember where he was. He lay quietly for a moment and then

He remembered that he had come to Grasse with Janine on what he felt was a wild goose chase. He admitted grudgingly to himself that his attraction to the strong willed CIA operative was part of the story. He slid out of bed and walked over to the connecting door between their rooms. He hesitated for a moment while his eyes grew accustomed to the darkness, then he tried the door. It wasn't locked. Perhaps Janine has been wondering about him too, and remembering how they had come together in Tunisia, like two people in an earthquake. Not able to get enough of each other. Now they were older and wiser, but her combination of toughness and humor still attracted him. He planned tonight to show her just how much.

The windows to her room were open and a faint light from the street filtered through the branches of the trees outside. She seemed to be sleeping soundly, there was no movement from the bed. The covers were bunched up in the middle and he couldn't see her face in the darkness. He slid into bed beside her reaching out a searching hand for her body, but there was nothing there, just a bunched up blanket that smelled of lavender. He jumped to his feet, swearing. Turning on the lights in the room, he saw that the door to the hallway was slightly ajar, and that her jacket was gone from the closet with her gun in it. He swore an oath and raced back into his room. She had done exactly what they had agreed not to do, she had gone back to the Hassan's without him, and in the middle of the night. It was a recipe for disaster, and he knew now that she was in the thick of it, alone.

****

When Janine came to, she was somewhere damp and cold. Her feet were bound and her hands tied behind her back. She was sitting on a rough cold floor that felt like stone. But she was in utter darkness, and alone. She felt behind her with her hands. She was on a cold rough surface.

The place smelled of ancient moisture as though it was underground. There was absolute silence. She might have been in a tomb. She felt a moment of regret that she hadn't told Rick where she was going. That had been stupid on her part. It was always smart to have backup in situations like this. But that was hindsight, and not much help in her present situation.

She wiggled on her butt across the cold stone floor. It was rough, as though she was sliding along ancient paving stones. A flicker of light came from high up above, and then it was gone. She was gagged, so she couldn't cry out, even if she had thought that it was a good idea. She knew that it wasn't. Whoever had trapped her might still be nearby. In fact, someone probably was. But where was she, in some kind of storage cellar under the house? It was too silent for that. She lifted her arms and felt a large bump on her head with her forearm. She had been knocked cold for sure. And she hadn't seen it coming. She had managed to wiggle as far as a rough, damp wall. She leaned against it for a moment, feeling dizzy and trying to get her bearings.

She could feel a rock sticking out from the wall and she slowly began to rub her bound hands against the protrusion, hoping to free herself. It was going to be hard work. Whoever had bound her had used thick, rough rope that didn't give easily. Her head ached, and the lump on her forehead began to throb with the beating of her heart. What had she gotten herself into? She heard a scratching, and a rodent ran across her foot and began to scratch at the floor near her, looking for food.

Now that her eyes were slowly getting used to the darkness, she could see objects in the room that looked like barrels. Perhaps she was in some kind of wine cellar. She hadn't seen one near the house, but that didn't mean that there wasn't one there. She heard a whimpering sound from the other side of the room and realized with shock that she was not alone. She could barely make out the shape of someone on the far side of the room, tied as she was and gagged. She hoped against hope that it wasn't the child. That would be too cruel. The little girl had done nothing but suppose that she was a ghost. Nothing to get her punished like this.

The moaning grew louder. Janine realized that it was someone trying to talk through a gag. She couldn't make out the words but it somehow gave her comfort to know that she wasn't alone, even if it did complicate the situations to have someone else to rescue besides herself. How she was going to do that she wasn't sure. She regretted again not telling Rick where she was going or what she planned to do. At the moment, she could certainly use some help.

****

Rick made his way on foot up the hill to the Hassan's property. It was dark except for a few dim perimeter lights that threw shadows across the lawn onto the front of the house. Grasse was certainly not a high crime area, there was no reason for strong security lights. That made his job of surveillance that much easier. But there was no sign of Janine, or of anyone else for that matter. If she had been foolish enough to come up here on her own tonight, there was no trace of her now. A bird fluttered down out of a tree dislodging some leaves that rattled down behind it. Then all was silent.

He heard voices coming in his direction, and moved behind the tree, standing quietly and hoping not to be noticed. If he was he had absolutely no excuse for being here in the middle of the night. 'Out for a midnight stroll' probably wouldn't wash as an excuse for the Hassans, who were already pretty suspicious about his and Janine's presence in the town.

The voices stopped and Rick froze in place. Then he could smell a cigarette and almost inhale its smoke. A tiny circle of light burned a few feet away. Now he could hear the men's voices clearly, speaking in Arabic. He didn't understand the language but he heard the bravado in their tones. They were clearly celebrating something. He hoped that it didn't have anything to do with capturing Janine, but her whereabouts still puzzled him. If she hadn't come here, then where had she gone in the middle of the night without telling him. That was just not good operative protocol. But then again, Janine wasn't known for following the rules. It was her greatest strength and sometimes her greatest failing. He feared that tonight it was the latter.

He followed the men back toward the house, which was in total darkness except for the few dim perimeter lights which cast weird shadows. The men sauntered, congratulating each other now in a mixture of French and Arabic. Rick caught the word 'prisoner,' and then one of the men made rude sucking sounds, and laughed evilly. Rick froze in his tracks. His instinct to grab the man by the neck and demand to know where Janine was hidden, was almost overpowering. He clenched his fists, touching the pistol in his pocket. But then a sound came from the house. A door opened abruptly and Hassan stood silhouetted against the light.

He spoke gruffly to the men in French, demanding that they shut their mouths. They were in enough trouble already. The situation had gotten out of hand. " If you have hurt the women, you will pay for it." he snarled. "We are supposed to turn them over intact if you remember, you fools." He spit out the last words as he gestured them into the kitchen.

The men followed sullenly. Their elation had turned sour. Whatever they were planning was now off limits for the moment. Rick was glad of that. But now more than ever he had to find 'the women,' hoping that Janine was not one of them. But he has a sinking feeling that she was. But where in the devil was she being held? And how was he going to find her?

He paced the perimeter of the property cautiously, looking for a lead. He silently examined the outbuildings, which were mostly locked for the night. There was no noise or light coming from any of them. He had seen their interiors on his daytime visit. They were really just working sheds. Not a place to hide a prisoner. Besides the workmen would be coming in the morning and opening everything up for the day's work. They must be holding Janine somewhere else, but within walking distance, as he hadn't heard the sound of a motor before he heard the men's voices coming from behind the main house.

He enlarged the perimeter of his investigation cautiously. But he was hampered by the dark and by walking on unfamiliar territory. Several times he tripped and almost fell over stumps of trees and debris that was left uncollected in heaps. When he reached a steep cliff at the rear of the property he heard a noise and froze, all of his senses alert. But it was the sound of a night bird of some kind, calling to its mate. Then a strong gust of wind hit him suddenly and he crouched down for a moment to get out of its debris laden path. Just then he thought he heard sounds that were not coming from the night sky, but from the hill behind him. The darkness was so complete that it was disorienting. He stayed crouched down, trying to control his breathing, straining his ears. But all he heard was velvet night silence broken only the sound of his own heart beating,

Chapter Thirty

Janine has managed to roll over onto her side, and inch her way along the floor toward the muffled noises on the other side of the cellar. She scratched her arms on the rough floor in the process as she snaked along. But through the faint light, she could see what looked like a bundle of rags on the other side of the room. The bundle was making strangled sounds much like crying. Whatever was there was clearly not an animal, as she had previously imagined, but a human being. A very unhappy human being from the sound it was making. Janine called out softly, "What is your name?" The sniffling grew more pronounced as the bundle sank into itself. Whoever was there was tied and gagged as she was, Janine was sure of it, but she had no idea how to get them both free, trussed up as she was like a Thanksgiving turkey.

Some of the large barrels were tipped over as though empty. Janine scooted over to one on her bottom and attempted to rub the ropes that held her hands against the metal rounds holding the broken barrel pieces together. All she succeeded in doing was further scraping her arms and wrists until they stung and bled profusely. She muttered a swear word in French and she thought that she heard the bundle echo in a muffled voice. Perhaps the bundle was human after all and as frustrated as she was!

Anger was better than despair in this situation, anger might get them free. Sobbing certainly wouldn't do it. By wiggling her chin until it almost dislocated her jaw, she managed to loosen the gag over her mouth. She used her voice cautiously, there was no guarantee that someone wasn't standing guard outside the door, ready to pounce if they heard the sound of voices. She moved nearer to the bundle, inching her way along the floor, feet first, crablike, for traction.

The bundle moved slightly as though trying to sit up straight against the wall. Janine could see that what she thought was rags was really a voluminous *abaaya* gray in color but covering its wearer from the crown of the head to the feet, which were also bound together as Janine's were. Only the eyes were visible, they were huge and lined with kohl and looked drugged or very frightened. The whimpering sounds continued, but now Janine could see that the robe had been taped with thick vinyl tape across where the mouth should be. Anything more than making muffled sounds was impossible. But the eyes told the story, they were wide and terrified, and female.

"I'm going to try to get us out of here," Janine whispered. " Are you able to stand?" The woman in the *abaaya* shook her head violently, sliding back down to the floor in a hopeless gray heap, her head almost touching the rough cement floor in her despair. Janine was nonplused How was she going to get herself out of this, not to mention this other woman who seemed to have totally given up. That was not Janine's nature. Her German mother had taught her to be tough and her CIA training had made her tougher.

Mostly because she had to compete with men in her training, who were only too anxious to see her fail.

But she hadn't reckoned on this kind of scenario when she had come out tonight to reconnoiter. Haddad must have been waiting for someone to sneak back to look the situation over again. Her capture had been too rapid and too well organized. For a fleeting moment, she even wondered if the child had been part of the scenario. She put that thought aside. It had been her own stupidity and overconfidence that had gotten her in to this. She wondered briefly what the woman in the *abaaya* had done to deserve a similar fate.

A strange thought crossed her mind. Could this huddled gray shape be the Princess? She couldn't believe that Hassan would treat Saroya like this. Her father was too powerful in the Arab world. She would certainly be worth more for a ransom than kept huddled like garbage in a dark basement. Unless they were trying to teach her a lesson. The ways of Arab justice when administered by men were very strange. Her thoughts were cut short by the sound of the door opening. A faint sliver of light crept into the room, with the acrid smell of a cigarette. It was Hassan himself coming to check on his prisoners. Janine lay perfectly still, hiding her bleeding hands behind her back. It wouldn't help to let him know that she was trying to untie herself. He addressed himself in Arabic to the gray bundle against the wall, asking the woman when she planned to cooperate with him, and tell him where she had hidden her jewels. He was clearly unaware that Janine understood every word.

So this must be Saroya and for some reason Hassan thought that she had hidden her jewelry somewhere and he was trying to find it. This puzzled Janine as she thought that she had seen most of it at Madam Zebur's shop. Unless those had been fake and Saroya had hidden the real jewels somewhere else to help her in her plans to escape. It was all very strange. The woman in the *abaaya* shook her head stubbornly, and stopped whimpering. Janine admired her guts since Hassan clearly had the upper hand.

"I will leave you here a little longer till you get cold and hungry enough to tell me the truth," he said, leaning over and hissing into her covered face. She stared back at him with large luminous eyes and shook her head in denial. He pulled his hand back as though to strike her, and then, as though thinking better of it, turned his attention for a moment to Janine, who was lying prone on the floor. He nudged her side with the corner of his boot, and getting no reaction, muttered a curse in Arabic and turned away, promising that he would return when they were colder and hungrier. "That is if the rats haven't gotten to you first," he said, with a nasty laugh, as he closed the door.

Janine breathed easier and continued to work on the ropes holding her hands. By taking most of the skin off her wrists she had almost managed to work one hand free. The rope burns stung terribly, but the note of menace in Hassan's voice spurred her on. Whatever the cost, she was not going to let him win. She had made more than one false move in this situation, but she wasn't going to make another. There was too much at stake.

Finally she pulled her bloody hands free and managed to reach the other woman. She pulled the strip of tape off her mouth and hurried to untie her hands. She had to hurry if they were going to escape before Hassan or his men returned. The woman mumbled a "thank you" in Arabic, while she hurried to untie her feet. She got up stiffly, still tangled in the voluminous *abaaya* which billowed around her like a parachute as she tried to stand. She was unsteady on her feet , as though she had been bound for a long time.

"Can you walk?" Janine asked in Arabic. The woman nodded and took a few hesitant steps toward the door. But it was secured tightly from the outside. Janine had heard the familiar sound of a bolt sliding into place as Hassan left, trailing his acrid cigarette smoke behind him. There was no window to be seen, as Janine moved around after freeing her feet. She could tell that they were in some sort of cave and not the basement of the building as she had first imagined. The walls were rough and damp and the only furniture a few old half broken barrels that might have once held wine. There was nothing to use as a weapon or to pry open the door. She turned her attention to the woman who was now drooping disconsolately on the door.

"Who are you, and what have you done to make Hassan so angry with you?" she asked in French, guarding the fact that she spoke and understood Arabic. The woman just shook her head as though she was too weary to talk, and continued to lean against the wall. Her eyes, though tear stained, were quite beautiful, although they continued to look terrified

" Do you think that they will kill us?" She asked in a trembling voice.

"Not if I have anything to do with it," Janine replied with a bravado that she didn't feel. She continued to search the room, looking for something that she could use as a weapon when Hassan or his men returned. She found a half broken metal bar and tested its weight in her hand. It might work in the dark for a moment, but only if one man came in at a time. It would be useless against two armed men. She had really painted herself into corner this time.

Chapter Thirty One

Rick continued to prowl around in the dark. He had heard someone approaching and had backed off far enough to see him enter a door in what appeared to be a cave in the side of the hill. He was too far away to know what was going on, but he could smell the acrid smoke of a strong French cigarette and hear the rumble of a man's voice. The man had left after a few minutes, obviously angry. Then he had heard the harsh sound of a bolt being slammed into place. He only hoped that there wasn't a padlock on the end of it. If he was going to see if Janine was being held inside, he had to get in and out quickly before anyone returned.

Moving cautiously, he sidled up to the door and felt along the metal bar that held the door in place. It was almost impossible to do in the dark and he didn't dare take the chance of lighting a match or the small flashlight on his key chain. Finding the bolt was an exercise in futility. He put his ear to the door and thought that he heard the sound of women's voices inside. He took a chance and knocked softly on the door three times, paused and then knocked three times again. There was dead silence inside and for a few minutes he thought that he had made a bad mistake. Janine might be in hiding somewhere else on the property, waiting for a chance to investigate. He ground his teeth in frustration. If he ever saw her again she would be lucky if he didn't wring her neck.

Then it came. Three tentative knocks on the oak door and then three more. Someone was certainly locked inside. And whoever it was wanted out. Now he had to figure out how to get the heavy bar off the door without making a loud noise. A noise that he suspected would bring someone that he didn't want to meet, crashing over to stop him.

The bar was heavy and slick with accumulated moisture. It fit into clumsy metal holders and then into a heavy metal bar that felt as though it had been built to keep out giants. He tried getting under it and pushing up, but it wouldn't budge. The need for speed and caution was evident, but he had neither for the moment. Another soft knocking came from inside and he answered it cautiously.

Finally the bar began to budge slightly. He tugged on it with all his strength and was rewarded to feel it slip up out of its metal keepers. He tried to pull the door open quietly, but it screeched on its ancient metal hinges. He could see two shadowy figures inside, one holding what looked like a formidable club. "Janine", he hissed, " If that's you, don't murder your rescuer."

He could hear a woman sobbing softly. But he was sure that it wasn't Janine. She was too tough for that. She led another figure through the open door, draped in a voluminous *abaaya* that obscured the size and sex of the occupant. Though Rick surmised that it was another woman. Janine half pushed, half led the figure through the door. Keeping a protective arm around it. The woman half stumbled and Rick reached out to help. The woman stopped in her tracks, as though frightened to continue forward. Janine spoke to her reassuringly and urged her to hurry. They could hear sounds of activity coming from the house, which meant that they didn't have any time to waste.

Rick put the heavy bar back on the door and closed it securely. But Janine kept her barrel stave in her free hand. It was the only weapon that she had at the moment, and it was better than nothing. Rick led them hurriedly through the underbrush the way that he had come. Giving the house a wide berth and working their way cautiously back to where Janine indicated that she had hidden their rented vehicle. The woman in the *abaaya* kept it clutched about her as though for protection, although it would have been much easier for her to walk without it. She seemed to want its protection and Janine didn't have time to argue. Her whole attention was now focused on getting through the underbrush before Hassan and his men returned to the cave to finish their bullying.

When they reached Janine's car, they loaded the *abaaya* clad figure into the back seat. A whispered "merci" was all they got for their trouble. Janine's ankles and wrists were still stinging from rope burns and she knew that the other woman must be just as uncomfortable, but she didn't make a sound. She huddled in the back seat like a gray ghost as Rick drove rapidly toward their guest house and relative freedom. "We need to get out of town a quickly as possible," Rick said under his breath. "You stay in the car while I get our stuff from our rooms. We can make it to Cannes in a few hours and take the train from there in the morning, after we regroup. I don't think that Hassan's thugs will follow us there."

"Don't be too sure," Janine whispered back " I think that we have someone with us that he wants very badly for reasons known only to himself. The more distance that we can put between ourselves and the Hassans tonight, the better."

While Rick hurriedly got their bags from their rooms and left a brief note on the reception desk explaining their quick departure as ' urgent business,' Janine attempted to talk to the woman in the back seat. But all attempts to question her were met with a shake of her head and downcast eyes. Janine decided that she was still in shock and to let her alone till they got to Cannes. But on his return, Rick had another idea. "I think that we had better drive to Marseilles. It's longer by a few hours but the station there is much larger and it will be easier to get lost in the crowd. Also we can get some other clothing for our passenger that will make her harder to spot."

"Or easier," Janine said obliquely. She was still not convinced of the identity of the woman that they had rescued. And it was made more puzzling by the woman's steadfast refusal to remove the veil covering half of her face. Her large dark eyes watched them solemnly, but she didn't seem any more trusting of them than she had been of Hassan and his men. Janine tallied it up to shock at the situation that she found herself in, and decided to just let her be until they got to their final destination. She had enough to do to ride shotgun for Rick and follow the map with the small flashlight he gave her from his key chain.

It was a relief to drive through the silent village past the Place Aux Aires with its splashing fountain and the silent Cathedral at the end of the square. Rick was driving without headlights and Janine held her breath that they wouldn't hit a wandering sheep or goat out for a midnight stroll. There was a faint moon now, illuminating their way, and as they started down the hill, Rick put on the dim running lights to see the twisting road better.

It was at that moment that they both heard the sound of a powerful motor coming rapidly closer. Glancing in the rear view mirror Janine could see a huge truck with blazing headlights coming down the hill behind them. It was gaining on them rapidly. Rick pushed their Citroen to the limit around the steep curves. Their vehicle was small and easy to manipulate but no match for the heavy truck behind them should it decide to run them down, or try to push them over a cliff.

The truck roared menacingly, pursuing them down the hill with a grinding of gears and blasts of its horn. It was like a monster chasing a fly. The Citroen took the downward curves wildly. Janine hung onto her seat as Rick gunned the motor, weaving back and forth from one side of the road to the other in an effort to avoid the truck. Once it got close enough to ram them, but then pulled back at the last minute. Janine surmised that Hassan's men had orders to take them alive. It would be too easy to push their small vehicle over a barrier into the valley below where they wouldn't be found for days, if ever. Between the swerving of the car from one side of the road to another, she searched the map frantically for an escape route.

Rick took a chance as he rounded a curve and headed into an unmarked side road, at the same time dousing his lights. It was a rough dirt track and not a road at all. They held their breath as the truck roared past them down the hill.

"Now what do we do?" Janine asked. "We certainly don't want to meet them at the bottom if they are who I think they are."

"Where does this track go?" Rick asked gruffly. "Does it even appear on the map?"

"As a thin red line," Janine whispered, "with the indication that it is 'often impassable in winter'. So what do we do now?"

"I guess we take the chance, since it isn't winter yet," Rick said, grimly. They were now on a narrow dirt track that was more a cow path than a road, that wound down the hillside in a leisurely fashion, complete with axle breaking bumps, till it reached the coast road sometime later. By then, they had all had their teeth rattled almost out of their heads. During all this time the woman in the back seat hadn't make a sound. Janine looked back once or twice to make sure that she was still there, she was so quiet. She found the woman sitting as though frozen, with her eyes tightly shut and her hands clutching the arm rests on either side of her.

"She probably wishes that she was back in the cave right now," Janine said softly. "Sometimes the terror you know is better than the one that you are afraid is coming. And she has no idea who we are. We could be just another set of kidnappers for all she knows."

"But we're not, and you risked your neck to get her out of there. I hope that she appreciates it." Rick answered, surveying the main coast road carefully in both directions before he drove off on it toward Marseilles. " I'm going to put some gas in this buggy before we go too much farther. Unfortunately it doesn't hold much in the tank. That's one of the reasons that it's so light."

They drove as far as they could before stopping to refuel, aware that Hassan's men could still be in front of them. Rick filled the tank as fast as he could while Janine kept watch.

"With any luck they've gone in the direction of Cannes to look for us. It doesn't make sense that we would drive all the way to Marseilles tonight." she said hopefully.

Rick shook his head. "Let's hope that they follow your logic. You grab some sleep if you can. We will change places every so often so that neither of us gets too groggy, and can spell the other off every hour or so."

Chapter Thirty Two

They drove into the old port of Marseilles just as the first light was breaking over the harbor. Fishermen were already getting the boats ready to go out for the day's catch as they had for hundreds of years. The light was serene and lovely. Both Janine and Rick were fighting to stay awake, after a night on the road. Two large *cafe aux lait* served in what looked like soup bowls, were a welcome sight. Their passenger was sound asleep, lying on the back seat of the car, seemingly exhausted.

Rick and Janine took their coffee at a small table outside by the parked car so that they could keep an eye on it and on her. " Now that we seem to have rescued her, for the moment, do you know who she is?" Rick asked over his steaming cup liberally laced with sugar.

"She may be Princess Saroya, or she may be someone impersonating her. It's strange that she hasn't tried to communicate with us. That tells me that something unorthodox is going on. Or that she is afraid of us too. She may think that we are just another part of the plot to kidnap her."

"What makes you think that maybe she isn't the Princess?" Rick said, almost sighing with delight as he bit into a baguette coated with jam.

" If it is Saroya, why wouldn't she be glad of our help?" Janine answered, grabbing another hot roll from the basket, and washing it down with steaming coffee.

"Because she may think that we are from her father or brother and that we are going to take her back. She may know about the reward. It's been in all the papers." Rick said, hastily grabbing the last warm roll..

They fell silent as the waiter replenished their coffee, glancing curiously at the sleeping figure in the back of the car. Rick paid the check quickly. There was no reason to arouse suspicion or to leave a trail in case Hassan's men were still following them.

Janine joined him in the car and they went in search of a shop where they could get their passenger some western clothes. There was still nothing open, so Janine settled for a rumpled skirt and blouse that she had in her suitcase. Hoping that they would fit the woman, who was much shorter than she was. Their passenger was now awake and looking around groggily, not recognizing where she was. Janine held up the skirt and blouse, but the woman shook her head violently, clutching her *abaaya* around herself, and firmly tightening her headscarf.

"This is going to be harder than I thought," Janine said grimly. "Stop the car somewhere where we can have a heart to heart talk about wardrobe. The *abaaya* just won't cut it on the train."

" Not in the condition its in anyhow," Rick answered. "It looks like she's been wearing it in a war zone."

"What are you saying about me?" the woman asked suddenly in French. "Where are you taking me?"

"Well, the mummy speaks," Rick muttered under his breath. " I think that you two girls better have a private talk before we try to get her on a train to Paris."

When Janine tried to reason with her, the woman shook her head firmly. "I will not remove my robe. It is my only protection." she said in French " I do not know who you are or who has sent you, If you wish me to travel with you without protest. Leave me dressed as I am."

"Well, it looks like we're going to take her on the train dressed as she is. There are many conservative Muslim women around Marseilles, " Rick said calmly. "Perhaps she will be safer on the train dressed as one."

So three desperate travelers boarded the early train for Paris. Janine kept their passenger in the ladies' room until Rick had bought first class tickets in a reserved coach, hoping that they could board at the last minute unnoticed. They mistakenly thought that they had made it successfully, occupying seats in the last row of the coach, near the door. The train was a *rapide,* which meant that it only made a few stops, with less chance of someone getting on to look for their passenger.

The woman was silent. She glanced at Janine occasionally, her eyes frightened but defiant. Janine tried to look encouraging and to engage her in conversation in French. The woman wouldn't answer at first about why she had been in Grasse and with the Hassans. But as the morning wore on, and Janine switched to speaking Arabic, the woman seemed to gain some confidence. She said that she had been promised 'protection' in Grasse. But she wouldn't say 'protection' from what, or whom.

Janine had her own ideas. And she tried them out carefully, one at a time so as not to frighten the woman and close down their tentative conversation. "Did you know Safi, their son?" she asked casually, looking directly into the frightened women's eyes.

Her eyes grew large with surprise, and she drew in breath sharply. "Do you know where he is?" she asked abruptly. "He promised to help me."

'Bingo', Janine thought, looking over at Rick who was pretending to be deep in a copy of Le Monde. "When did you last see him?" Janine asked casually, trying not to appear too eager for the information.

"When he dropped me off at his parents' house," the woman whispered. "He was called back to Jordan suddenly, so he left me in his father's care. Then everything went wrong."

"They wanted money not to tell where you were?" Janine suggested casually. Not wanting to appear to lead her on.

The woman nodded, "But I had given away my jewelry, I had nothing else to pay then with to keep silent. But they didn't believe me."

Janine nodded understandingly, "It is often that way when you trust people too soon."

"But I have known Safi for a long time," the woman protested. "He was my father's pilot, but my friend. He said that he could help me."

"But instead, he turned you over to his family to get money." Janine said in mock indignation.

"No, it wasn't like that." The woman said, suddenly very upset. "He was my friend. He promised to help me get to America, where I would be free."

Janine leaned back in her seat. So that was the carrot that has led her into this mess, a passage to the States. It didn't matter how poor or rich they were they all wanted the same thing. The magic trip to a place they thought would solve all their problems and set them free.

"But how was he going to get you there?" Janine asked, curiously. "It takes a visa and a passport to get you into the States. Do you have one somewhere?"

The woman shook her head. " I don't know anymore. Safi was going to get all those things for me and arrange the transportation. That is what my jewelry was for. I gave everything to Madame Zebur to sell for the money for the passport in her daughter's name. That way they would think that I was a French citizen and there would be no trouble with my father tracing me."

Janine nodded. It was a plan that might have worked, Soroya and Madame Zebur's daughter looked enough alike to be sisters. But she knew that the jewelry hadn't been sold. She had seen Madame Zebur's models wearing some of it. She even had one of the gold bracelets in her possession. The girl had been thoroughly tricked. There was never going to be a trip to America. But she hesitated to tell her that in her confused state. Instead Janine decided to probe a little further. " Do you have friends in America?"

For the first time the woman's eyes shone. Janine was convinced now that the woman was Saroya.

"Oh yes, I have a friend at NYU, the University in New York. His name is Keith. He will arrange everything for me when I arrive." Then she looked frightened, as though she realized suddenly that she might have said too much.

The train slowed for its first brief stop and a vendor came through the train selling coffee and soft drinks. Janine asked Saroya if she would like something to drink since she hadn't had any breakfast. The woman declined, but said that she needed to visit the toilet just behind them in the coach. Janine stood up to let her by and moved over to talk to Rick and tell him what she had just learned. He was congratulating her on her investigative techniques when the train slowly began to move out of the station. Saroya had not yet returned, so Janine went to the door of the restroom and knocked softly. There was no answer but the door was unlocked. Janine pushed the door open slowly so as not to disturb its occupant. The restroom was empty but the rest room floor was covered with a crumpled gray *abaaya.*

Janine rushed to look out the window. The train had now picked up speed and there was no sign of Saroya on the rapidly receding platform A black sedan was speeding away in the opposite direction. It was as if Saroya had disappeared into thin air. If it hadn't been for the crumpled *abaaya* that Janine was holding in her hands, she might have believed that the woman had never existed. How had she gotten off the train so suddenly? Had someone been able to trace them and follow them onto the train just waiting for an opportunity to snatch the Princess at the first train stop? Janine kicked herself for not being more vigilant.

Whoever was after the woman was very determined and exceedingly well organized to have known where they had gone and which train they had taken. But it didn't matter now. She slumped down in the seat beside Rick, "The pigeon has flown the coop or been snatched" she said, showing him the gray *abaaya.* "I found this in the restroom after the train started."

"You think that she is running around naked?" Rick asked incredulously. " That doesn't fit in with Saudi modesty."

"She was probably was wearing a designer gown underneath, maybe one of Madame Zebur's creations. She just didn't want us to see it. Anyhow now what do we do next?"

"Follow the money," Rick said thoughtfully, "Who stands to make the most by turning her in to her brother?"

"I have an idea," Janine said thoughtfully, "and when we get to Paris that is exactly where I am going. In the meantime I've got to figure out what if anything I'm going to tell them back at the office," she muttered, stretching out in the seat beside Rick. "Essentially, I stuck my neck out to find her, and then lost her again. That will give the 'boys' a lot to chuckle over at my expense."

"But think about it from her side for a minute," Rick said thoughtfully. "If you had taken her in to the French authorities, they would have handed her over to her brother or his representative and she would be loaded onto a plane to Saudi Arabia right away to endure the wrath of her father."

"All for the love of a boy named Keith, who goes to NYU. Wonder how she met him," Janine said yawning and leaning her head back against the seat. She didn't wake up until the train reached Paris and the Gare De Lyon. It was late afternoon, thankfully, too late to call her office and check in. That gave her the evening to think about how she was going to present her story. There was no chance of finding out where they had taken the Princess. Whoever had taken her off the train, with or without her consent, had done it too rapidly and cleverly to leave an obvious trail. Right now she was ready for a hot bath and a change of clothes, in her apartment on Rue Belle Chasse.

She said good night to Rick at the station and thanked him for his help, refusing his offer of a drink and dinner. He was really a nice man, she realized, a good person to have around in an emergency, but for now she longed to be alone and to lick her wounds. She had taken a chance on a wild hunch, and now she was going to have to pay for it one way or another. But she would think about that in the morning. Right now, her apartment called out to her, promising the comfort of solitude.

But it was not to be. Her phone was ringing off the hook as she opened the door and her message tape was full. Obviously her boss at the office had been looking for her and his message was now grim. "Get in here and tell us where you have been. The Saudi government is launching a protest against you and your unorthodox means of searching for the Princess."

Janine shook her head. This was all she needed now. To be held responsible for the Princesses abduction, when she had been the one trying to bring her in safely. What fools these men were. She felt like turning in her resignation, as she often did. And then, thought better of it, when she realized that she only had a few more years to go to exit graciously.

She returned the phone call to the office and held the receiver away from her ear as her boss berated her. It seemed that the Saudis were claming that she and an accomplice had kidnapped the Princess and were spiriting her away, when they had intervened just in time to save her. They said they had the Princess's own testimony to prove it.

"Well, as you can imagine, that is not the case," Janine answered wearily. "To begin with, what would I do with a Saudi Princess? Government regulations prevent me from accepting a reward for finding her. Is it possible for you to accept the fact that I was just doing my job?"

"Somewhat outside the lines of your assignment it seems," her boss answered sarcastically. "Get yourself and your accomplice in here first thing in the morning and your explanation better be good. This could mean your career," he finished ominously.

"Yeah, yeah, yeah," Janine said after she hung up the phone, she was weary to the bone of the Agency. If you succeeded it was just what was expected of you, and if you failed, all hell broke loose. She had no idea how to explain what had happened with the Princess. Haddad must have alerted the Saudis, for the reward, and given them an idea of how to track her to Marseilles. It had been a very slick operation and one that she should have anticipated if she hadn't been so tired.

She drew a hot bath and sank into it with relief. Sometimes she did her best thinking in a tub of scalding water doused with bath salts. There were so many pieces of this puzzle that didn't add up. Was the Jordanian pilot really trying to help Saroya or had he too been a part of an elaborate plot to disgrace her? Although she had certainly helped the plot along by linking up with an American, who seemed to have caught her fancy. Running way to America to be with him seemed pretty risky by itself. But she was perhaps young enough and foolish enough to try it.

Janine's knowledge of Saudi women was pretty sketchy, but she suspected that because of their restricted upbringing they were somewhat naïve, when it came to cross cultural love affairs.

She may even have convinced her father's favorite pilot, Safi Hassan, that she was in love with him to get his help. Any scenario was possible. It was a never-ending puzzle and one that she was too tired to wrestle with anymore tonight.

She fell into bed and into a troubled sleep. In her dream she was back in the cave with Saroya but this time the woman was wearing a sparkly abaaya and was covered with precious jewelry. She was taunting Janine, who was still manacled, telling her that it was all a game and that Janine had been taken in by it. She was free now and was going to do what she pleased with her life. Everything that she had told Janine was lies and half truths. Then she laughed tauntingly, flashing her bejeweled wrists and her fingers covered with diamond rings.

Janine awoke covered with sweat. Had the whole thing been a set up and was she the one who had been taken it by it, in her misguided attempt to do good? She scribbled the outline of the dream on a pad beside her bed so she would remember it in the morning to analyze it, then fell back into a sound sleep.

Chapter Thirty Three

She awoke the next morning with an absolute conviction that someone was trying to pull her strings. She wasn't sure who it was, so she dressed very carefully for her interview with her boss and the powers that be from the Saudi Embassy. Her standard black silk pants suit with a white shirt and black pumps should do it. She decided not to call Rick. There was no point in getting him more involved, unless her office absolutely demanded it. She was perfectly willing to take the blame herself for whatever story the Princess and or the Saudis had cooked up. It was not possible that anyone could honestly believe that she was involved in an abduction.

But she was wrong. When she got to the office she was greeted by a grim faced senior officer, flanked by legal counsel. The Saudi's were represented by a small dark skinned man, with a large leather briefcase who spoke halting English. The Princess was not there.

Janine was allowed to tell her story first. She skipped most of the details of her own capture, focusing on her rescue of the Princess and their subsequent trip to Paris on the train when the Princess had unaccountably disappeared. " As you may remember," Janine said politely. " My assignment was to locate the Princess using whatever means I thought necessary. That is exactly what I did."

"But without informing this office of where you were going or what you suspected had happened to her." her boss said firmly, glancing at the Saudi.

"I wasn't sure of the lead and as you can see on my record, I took personal time to investigate it. I found the Princess a prisoner of the Hassan's in Grasse at their essential oils factory. I liberated her and was bringing her to Paris when she unaccountably disappeared from the train."

"That is not possible," the Saudi said unctuously. "It was Hassan who alerted our Embassy that she was on the train. That is how our security service rescued her."

"What will happen to her now?" Janine asked, curious despite herself.

"That is not your affair," the Saudi said contemptuously. "It is enough for you to know that she will be returned safely to her family."

"And you will be put on immediate suspension until we resolve this matter," her boss said firmly. "It's clear to me that you were way out of line on this one."

"So do I turn in my badge or what?" Janine asked, too flippantly for her own good.

Her boss glared at her. "We will discuss that in private as soon as we are sure that the Saudi government is satisfied with our resolution of the matter."

The Saudi hoisted his large briefcase in leaving and spoke contemptuously over his shoulder. "Since this woman has diplomatic immunity, I will leave the appropriate punishment to your office. The Princess will be flown home today by her father's personal pilot, who has just returned from an important assignment in Jordan." Then looking suddenly as though he had already said too much, he scurried out of the room closing the door firmly behind him.

Janine's boss broke into a slight grin as the man left and shook his head. "The Saudis get what they want and we get blamed, or at least you do. It's a perfect diplomatic solution."

"You mean I'm not suspended?" Janine said in disbelief. That seemed too good to be true.

" Why don't you just make yourself scarce for a month without pay, till this all blows over and try not to get into any more difficulty during that time. Then we'll see. Once the Princess is safely at home, hopefully this will all be forgotten." He shook his head in disbelief. " Whatever game the Saudi's are playing, I'm sure that you didn't try to kidnap the Princess, that's not your style. Kill her perhaps, but not kidnap her," he finished ruefully, indicating the interview was over.

Janine walked out into the crisp autumn air with a spring in her step. She had a month's leave in her favorite city at her favorite time of the year. What could be better? She wasn't worried about Saroya once she heard that Safi Hassan was flying her back home. She would take money on the fact that an emergency stop in the American Virgin Islands or somewhere else close, would be made, even though it was far out of the direct route to Saudi Arabia. But there was no accounting for winds and storms these days.

Nothing like the storm that would take place in the palace once the King found out that he has lost both his daughter and his favorite pilot, and that neither one of them planned to ever return home.

Two small Arab boys came up close behind her as she walked. She shooed them away and then watched them closely as they ran off in another direction.

She followed them with her eyes. Where were they going and what were they up to? She shook her head and walked determinedly in the opposite direction. She had a month off and she was going to enjoy every minute of it, at least for a couple of days.

Epilogue

Two olive skinned people walked along the beach, hand in hand. The woman was very beautiful, with flowing dark hair and almond eyes. She wore a conservative one piece, black bathing suit, somewhat out of place on this tropical island, where most of the women were in scant bikinis. The man was tall with touches of gray at his temples and a proud military bearing.

The man couldn't take his eyes off the woman. He walked beside her protectively and watched her every movement jealously. He had just sacrificed his career for her and perhaps in the long run, his life. But every moment with her now was worth it. He had loved and admired her since she was a gawky teenager, teasing him from the back of her royal father's airplane.

He knew that his time with her was limited. But however long it was, it was precious to him. He would give his life for her. It was enough for him to give her, her life and freedom. Whatever time Allah gave him with her now was enough. She was and always would be, his Princess.